The Vendetta Killer

Book One Ashes to Ashes

By: Greg Carter

I want to thank all those in my life who supported me during the time I was writing this book. Otherwise I wouldn't have been able to craft this thrilling novel. You have my undying gratitude.

<u>Chapter 1 Fire</u>

It always started with fire and always ended with fire. There was something purifying, yet destructive about it. As a boy he would stare into its flickering flames for hours on end; feeling its warmth dance across his young skin, like playful shadows on the barren walls long overdue for a fresh coat of paint.

Every time was like the first; exciting, sensual, burning his soul, igniting a powerful yearning deep within. It was in a hidden, unexplored place, deep within the mysterious depths of his mind. Throughout the years he asked himself; why, why had fire become his life? No answer ever came, there never was. He was who he was without any regret; his curse unto death.

The memory of his first time ran through his mind as clear as mountain spring water. The screams of his enemy broke the calm silence of the darkness, like thunder booming in the heavens above on a beautiful storm-filled night. He was deliriously drunk with an incomprehensible ecstasy. A drug addict filled with a fire-induced erotic orgasm, set in motion by the roaring flames blistering the skin of the sick bastard who had been his demon; his torment, his fanatical obsession. Now in the end, only ashes would be left of the murderous scum who delighted in the torment of others.

"Scream you son-of-a-bitch; scream in agony; scream for mercy; mercy you showed no one," Sam shrieked, taunting him in his final seconds of life. He learned the secrets of fire long ago. There was nothing it couldn't destroy if it was hot enough.

It was always the same every time he woke up in the middle of the night soaked in sweat, drenched with memories of his past. Was he the man in his nightmares; or were they just twisted ramblings of a malfunctioning brain? One permanently damaged by the accident that robbed him of so much of his past and now threatened to take away his future?

Was his brain injury he suffered ten years ago a convenient excuse to forget his terrible past? Could he live with himself if he knew the truth? Was he a monster? Were his children; marriage, friends, even his job a vain attempt for redemption? He kept telling himself over and over, he was not the man in his nightmares. The one who delighted in the fiery agony of others? He was not the man who took such exquisite pleasure in any suffering; after all he wouldn't harm a fly; would he?

There was only one way to find out. He had to make the journey, a trip back to where it happened, where the demons haunt and forever linger in the depths of his forgotten past. He knew it would be a painful quest to remember, one he was loath to begin and unsure he could finish. Would it consume him? Would it take his life in the end? Would it give him the answers he so desperately needed? If Sam's life was ever going to have true meaning, he had to know the truth no matter how appalling.

It had been ten years since his accident. He was thirty years old when it happened on that hot summer day of July, 15 of 2001. One of the few things he could remember was the day and even the time; two p.m. He was running a crane on a construction site just outside of Columbus, Ohio in Hilliard. The load he was lifting suddenly shifted due to a gust of wind and caused the crane to collapse on top of him.

There were mangled pieces of steel everywhere; men ran in all directions when they heard the boom of the crane emit a god-awful screeching sound. They knew it meant run like hell and hope you're out of the way before it all came down on your head.

Unfortunately sitting in the enclosed cab Sam never had a chance to run like hell. He was barely able to get the door open before being entombed in the mangled wreckage of the towering crane. The last things he remembered were men shouting; sirens wailing, blurry faces of people working to pull his helpless body out of the crane's smashed cab.

He remembered bits and pieces after that, little things like the salty taste of his own blood. The heat and brightness of the late afternoon sun radiating down upon his swollen eyes. The nauseating smell of diesel pouring from the busted fuel tank; so many things about that day, yet ten years later much of his life was still lost to him. He could remember being in the Army, and images of a few people and places. He wasn't sure if they were his memories or just ones people told him. After all he had an amazing ability to make up memories because someone told him something that happened. Hell he didn't know if they did or didn't and could give a damn less.

Sam tried to remember people and places, or other things like his high school, yet no real memories ever came to him. Sam hated when he ran into people who knew him from his past. They would walk up to him and treat him like an old friend or family member when he had no idea who the hell they were. He quickly learned to fake it and when he couldn't, he would tell them about his brain injury and he couldn't remember like he use too.

Yet some people could not, or would not leave things alone. It was like pulling rusty nails with a crowbar. This was when he got angry and would find any reason to stop talking and get the hell out of there, before he said something to hurt their feelings. He knew they were only 'trying to help', but damn all he wanted was to be left alone.

His family never pushed him, never seemed

concerned about whom or what he remembered, only that he was alive and knew who he was. They didn't care if he couldn't remember any of his high school years or for that matter much of his childhood. They had him alive and that was good enough for them; others needed to take a lesson from them.

Sam had done well for himself, having grown up in a tough neighborhood. His father worked as a day laborer for construction companies around Columbus before starting his own. Sam joined the army right after high school and served in the first gulf war and when he came home he went to work as a crane operator in his father's construction business. The pay was extremely good and after all the business would be his one day.

He could still remember the proud look on his father's face the first day he came to work. His dad even changed the name of the company to Stout & Sons Construction Company, although Roger, Sam's brother didn't work in the company. That was eight years before his accident at the tender age of twenty-two. Of course after spending four years in the army he was ready to settle down, yet he could never find the right time or woman. So he was content to be single, simply enjoying life.

That was all before the accident, after which came the hard reality that life wasn't a given. You never knew if you were going to be alive one day or the next; hell for that matter the next minute. Sam had a few close calls in Iraq, but he never thought about dying, that was something that happened to others not him. At thirty years old he found himself fighting for life when a typical everyday turned into a real life nightmare.

It took him two years of therapy to recover from his injuries; it was during the last six months of which he met his wife. She was a physical therapist who replaced his former one, Arlene who didn't show up to work again. All her co-workers gossiped about how she had run off with a guy she had been talking to on the internet for the last month. Arlene was a pretty woman; mid-thirties, slightly overweight with short brown hair and brown eyes to match, pleasant conversations, yet she wasn't his type.

Now Jacquelyn her replacement on the other hand was quite a looker to say the least. She was around five foot seven, one hundred thirty pounds, gorgeous red hair and green eyes a man could get lost in and an extremely nice build which anyone who saw her knew she took great care of herself.

He enjoyed his sessions with her, even though she tortured him more than Arlene had if that were possible. Every time she would get close to him to help him stretch or whatever hellish exercise they were doing he would always sneak a smell. She smelled so divine with a hint of lavender and warm vanilla on her soft creamy white skin. He was extra careful not to get caught, although he noticed her smiling a few times when she thought he wasn't looking.

After he learned she was single, he worked up the courage to ask her out. To his disappointment she refused on the grounds she didn't date patients. However she made him a deal that once he was done with his therapy she would go out with him. He thought about asking for a different physical therapist, but knew that would piss her off and blow any chance he had with her.

He redoubled his efforts and finished in six months' time to everyone's amazement, who thought he had at least another year left. Jacquelyn was so impressed by his determination she went out with him the day after he left the Three Oaks Rehabilitation Center. She told him she never met a man who made such an effort to go out on a date with her. Six months after that they were married, and just after their first anniversary their daughter Cassandra was born.

A beautiful girl who took after Jacquelyn, according to Sam; two years after that, Sammy was born and the family was complete. At age forty Sam had been married for eight years with a seven year old daughter and a year five old son who was a spitting image of his father.

It was shortly after his fortieth birthday when the nightmares began. At first they were short, like fleeting snapshots; then they grew into nothing short of the worst horror flick you ever saw. He was afraid to talk to anyone about them, let alone his loving wife, it might freak her out. His doctor had already diagnosed him with bi-polar mania; post-traumatic stress disorder, and depression. He certainly didn't want to pop another damn pill and deal with even more side effects.

So he resorted to sleeping on the couch whenever the nightmares would wake him. Jacquelyn often ask why; he'd lie and tell her he was hurting; shoulder, neck, back, or some other made up ailment. He felt bad about lying to her, but what else could he to do; tell her he dreamed of roasting some imaginary man he hated.

Often she would tell him it was the stress of work and family life and he should take some time off. Which was the last thing he wanted or needed to do; that would surly drive him insane. If he was who he thought he was, he had to find some way of redemption. He'd already begun working on a plan, after finding one of the bodies in his dreams. If he was a monster, he had to find a way to redeem his soul; *kill those who deserved it* was his first thought. He could start with murders; then rapists, and child molesters. That would be one way to make amends for any evil acts he had committed in the past.

He had never harmed a child to his knowledge, but with his damaged memory how could he be sure? How could he be sure of anything? It's one thing when someone tells you you're a good person and a whole different thing to know for yourself.

He wondered many times in the past month about turning himself in and telling the cops about the dream that led him to an unmarked grave were he found a body. They would most certainly lock him up and throw away the key, glad he provided them a scapegoat to close an unsolved case. He couldn't stand the thought of being away from Jacquelyn and his kids.

Sam wondered if he had become psychic after the accident. The doctors told him the left side of his brain had been severely damaged in the accident and the right side would over compensate due to it. They told him he may be better in math; painting, and music owing to the fact the left brain is the logical part and the right brain deals with the abstract world. He did pick up painting afterwards as a hobby though his eyesight had been affected, before it was a perfect twenty-twenty and afterwards he had to wear glasses.

Could a damaged brain make you psychic though? And if you were, did that mean the dead would talk to you? He could not and would not resign himself to being a killer, as least not without reason; like the war were he had to kill, but they were the enemy. There were no feelings of hatred, he done what he had to do to survive period.

<u>Chapter 2 Demons In The Night</u>

Late one night while everyone slept; he awoke after another nightmare and finally decided it was time to go back to the body again. It was a cool autumn night of late September, the ground beneath his feet was wet from an earlier rain. The smell of damp leaves lingered in the midnight air when his shovel grated against bone. He gently removed the rest of the dirt from the corpse and there she lay, just like the first time he saw her. How many times would he have to come out and do this, before he made himself believe it was real?

Just like the dream, her boney fingers were still clutching an old moldy black purse, long black strands of hair flung wildly about the remains of her skull. Due to the decomposition of the body he had no idea how to tell the sex of it, he assumed it was a woman due to the clothes; long hair and purse. He didn't even know how to determine the cause of death; however it wasn't hard to imagine foul play had been involved. No one gets buried in a makeshift grave underneath an oak tree in an abandon industrial park on the outskirts of the city. Not unless someone wanted your body not to be found; no this had to be murder, no question about it.

The ghastly sight and ungodly smell caused him to turn his head and throw up the remains of his late dinner; it had tasted great going down, not so much coming back up. *Damn it man get a hold of yourself, now you've left your DNA everywhere.* Sam mentally cursed wiping his mouth on the sleeve of his blue flannel shirt. He regained his composure and looked back into the shallow grave with his flashlight.

Okay, time to see if this psychic stuff is real, he thought. He laid the flashlight on the side of the grave and leaned the shovel on the mound of excavated earth. He took both his hands and worked them in a circular motion one over the other, closed his eyes and concentrated on the woman lying in front of him. Nothing happened; he opened his eyes feeling like a complete fool and not to mention a total waste of time. God he was really going insane if he thought he could talk to the dead. He never believed in such things, even though he loved to read books about it, Halloween was his favorite holiday.

Without warning two skeletal hands shot upward in a blink of an eye grabbing each side of his face and pulled him downward. In that split second a pulse of blue light caused his body to go limp. Then in his mind he saw a vision of a heavy set man, dark hair and beard coming at him with a long sharp knife; he was going to kill him. However when he screamed it came from a woman's body, he was seeing the killer from her point of view. When he came to, he was lying face to face on top of the dead body.

He jumped to his feet as fast as he could and hurried to recover the shallow grave. It was 1:30 a.m. he knew he had to get home before anyone woke up and missed him; thankfully his wife was a heavy sleeper due to her medication she took to help her sleep.

A million questions went through his mind as he was driving home in his old red pickup. Should he turn himself in? For what; dreams? Should he tell the police where the body is? He would have to wait a while now; if they took soil samples they might find his DNA.

In the meantime he had seen the killer and it wasn't him, at least for this poor woman he wasn't. Should he try to send an anonymous letter to the police about the location of the body? Maybe he could find the find the bastard and kill him? How? He didn't have any idea of whom it was, *wait for more visions* he thought, and then plan it out so he wouldn't get caught.

He learned a lot by watching loads of detective shows, he could cremate the remains that way they wouldn't be able to determine the cause of death. Yet he would have to provide them with something of the killer's so they could identify him. Maybe he would spread the killer's ashes over the victim's grave and leave a note telling them what the killer done and provide a little piece of him for DNA to prove it. He didn't have a lot to go on though; he had only seen the killer's face through the victim's eyes.

The drive back to his house didn't take long. All the lights were still off when he pulled into the driveway. He quickly shut the truck off and quietly let himself into the house being careful not to make any noise. He wasn't worried about Jacquelyn hearing him, just the kids and if they woke up they would surely wake her up. He left his muddy boots in the truck to avoid making a mess and headed straight to the bathroom to wash and change into his night clothes.

He looked over at the clock, it read 2:30 a.m. Damn six o'clock is going to come early he thought getting into the position he always slept in. He could already feel his body aching from the stress of the night's encounter and knew he would pay come morning. Nowadays it was alien to him to go without pain which had been his companion for the last ten years. Sam reached into the drawer of his night stand and grabbed his bottle of pain pills and popped two. They tasted so bitter without water to swallow them, but that just reminded him of life. Most of the time he would wait until the pain was too much to bear before taking any, because he was afraid of becoming an addict. However the pain medicine made him feel like his old self, even if it was for a few short hours.

Before the accident he had been a healthy athletic thirty year old, who lived life to its fullest. He was a handsome, six foot two, dark brown hair and hazel eyes never had any trouble with the ladies. He hadn't changed much in the last ten years, maybe not as muscular as he once was. He still had a head full of rich brown hair with no gray and a great smile or so he was told. Inwardly he always felt insecure; he never thought of himself as anything other than ordinary.

His younger brother Roger was always jealous of him. When they would to go out clubbing he would always wind up with the hottest girl. It wasn't Sam's fault; he took after his dad and his grandfather who had a great head of hair. Roger started going bald at twenty-five, which he blamed on their mother's father. Roger used everything he could to stop it, of course nothing worked so he simply shaved it clean and made jokes about it so no one else could. Roger done well; not wanting to work in the family business he started his own restaurant and already opened his tenth one.

Sam was so proud of Roger and tried to tell him, although he still felt Roger was jealous of him. Last time they talked Roger made a comment of how he would like to be happily married like he was. If he only knew the demons his brother had to carry around. The never ending pain and now on top of it all, this new terror.

Sam had to figure out what to do about things. Did the brain injury make him crazy? After all who in their right mind would think of killing people, even if the ones you're killing are evil monsters who hurt, maim and kill. Sure he killed people in war, but they were the enemy and it was his job. After all when you're in the infantry it doesn't take you long to figure out what you're going to be doing in combat. He'd seen dead bodies littering the battlefield, mangled remains of soldiers and civilians blown apart by air strikes and artillery; yes he had seen his share of death.

Soon the effects of the pills called out to him like an old friend waiting to see him again; though he didn't share the same enthusiasm.

The nightmares came again, first the fiery one followed by the bearded man with the knife. Why was he the killer in one and the victim in the other? Could he be killing the bearded murderer in the first dream? Why would he want to kill anyone after Desert Storm? He had seen enough death to last a life time, which was why he never re-enlisted. All those poor lost souls, who through no fault of their own were caught in the middle of something far larger than themselves. He had seen the fear in their eyes when he walked the streets of the towns they were fighting in to clear out Saddam's Republican Guard, many of whom fought like hell. He felt sorry for the innocent civilians' trapped in-between.

"Good morning sleepy head," he heard the soft whisper of his wife's voice in his ear.

"What time is it? Am I late?" Sam asked quickly, trying to get his bearings.

"Settle down, I called your father and told him I was letting you sleep in. He wants you to take the day off and I already took the kids to school; coffee's brewing," Jacquelyn said smiling.

"You know if you weren't so damn beautiful, I'd be mad you let me sleep in," Sam grinned.

"Now now potty mouth," she said, wagging her index finger at him like a disapproving mother.

"Sorry dear, but you are pretty damn beautiful; now come here," Sam said as he grabbed her and pulled her down on top of him kissing her passionately.

"You're forgiven," she said breathlessly.

"That's more like it," he laughed. "Up for some morning fun?"

"Oh I love your style," she said already undressing. It was rare to have the kids out of the house and home alone early enough not to be worn out. The sex was hotter than usual leaving both of them lying there panting.

"Wow, babe I swear you just keep getting better and better," Sam breathed heavily.

Jacquelyn rolled over smiling as she closed in for a kiss. "All you baby, all you," and then she kissed him so passionately it sent chills all the way to his toes.

"Do you have to work today babe?" Sam asked.

"Sorry hun, I told Jenny I'd fill in for her so she could take her son to the doctor. Did you need anything?" she asked heading for the shower.

"No I thought we might go out for lunch or something," he said a little deflated.

"How about Thursday?" she asked.

"Deal," Sam smiled.

"Now I want you to relax and don't worry about anything. Tracy is going to pick up the kids from school and watch them at her house until I get off. I want you to take a day for yourself," Jacquelyn told him before going to shower.

The one thing he loved the most was her amazing ability to take such great care of him. She knew him well enough to know when he was over doing it and when to step in and take charge without bulldozing over him. Well at least he could use today to get some things planned out.

The first thing he was going to do was figure out exactly what was going on with the visions. Then an idea jumped into his mind about a sign he'd seen driving to work. There was a small white house with a large sign in the front lawn offering spiritualists consultations. That would be a good place to learn about what's happening to him.

He waited until she was out of the shower and dressed; and then kissed her goodbye before getting ready and heading out himself.

Chapter 3 Detective Colburn

He always dreamed of getting into the homicide division, yet getting there was proving to be a major pain in the ass. He had joined the police academy just out of high school and after six years of pounding the traffic beat worked his way onto the vice squad. Everything came harder for him; he was the first cop in his family, so he couldn't rely on inside connections for any help. When he finally made it, he was proud of the fact that it was him and him alone who done it. However getting on the vice squad was like starting over at the bottom again.

On the traffic beat he had earned a measure of respect as a hardworking patrolman you could count on to pull his own weight and not let you down. Here again he had to prove himself all over, it was frustrating to say the least, but this would hopefully be the last step he would have to take to get into the homicide division.

After making detective his new Captain thought he needed a little 'seasoning' as he put it before being put on homicide. What the hell was he a fucking turkey? Captain Harris wouldn't know a crime if it bit him in his fat ass, which he sat on all day in his office. He probably hadn't been in the field in twenty years, yet James had to bite his tongue and take what he dished out so he could make homicide.

Then after that, he wouldn't see that fat bastard enough to care what he thought. Just because he was only twenty-five didn't mean he was 'wet behind the ears' like the others said when making fun of a rookie. Some of the older cops could be downright obnoxious to the younger ones on the force. To James they were all there to do the same job, which was simple enough, stop criminals. A little hazing was to be expected, hell they were guys after all, well women too, but to him when you were in uniform there was no such thing as gender.

"Well congratulations Detective James A. Colburn!" A booming male voice behind him loudly proclaimed; which he recognized immediately as Larry his buddy from the traffic beat.

"That's right and you better watch your step or I'll run your ass in. Now come on over here and buy me a cup of coffee," James said with a fake look of being serious.

"My my, cocky aren't we," Larry said laughing as he sat down across from him in the old vinyl booth. It was a family run dinner on the edge of town, good food at decent prices.

"So how's detective life treating you?" Larry asked.

"Oh, you know hob-knobbing with the rich and powerful. Captain's getting me a BMW for a squad car next week. Hell at this rate I'll probably get a pay raise too," James said sarcastically.

"That good, huh?" Larry said raising an eyebrow.

"May I take your order, officer?" A cute young blond haired waitress asked as she stood by the table with her pen and pad in hand.

"Cup of coffee please, black no cream and whatever your lunch special of the day is," Larry told her without even turning to look at her.

"And you sir?" She turned to James who just then realized the reason she didn't call him officer was because for the first time in six years he was in plain clothes. He was always use to being called officer when he was getting lunch while working.

"Oh, refill on the coffee please, cream and I'll go ahead and have a cheese burger with mayo, bacon and tomato, and order of fries too. Thanks," James ordered then turned back to Larry and waited till the girl left.

"What the hell was that all about? You wouldn't even look at her." James asked keeping his voice low.

"Well you know me and Cindy been having trouble and I'm trying to do better," Larry said.

"By not looking at a waitress?" James asked confused.

"No dumb-ass, Cindy caught me cheating and I promised if she'd take be back, hell would freeze over before I'd even look at another woman."

"Yea but damn Larry she's only a waitress, are you planning to throw her on the table and have sex with her right here and now?"

"Fuck you James, you know I got kids man, I can't let them down. I got to keep my dick in my pants or else," Larry said agitated.

"Ok man I'm sorry, I didn't know things had gotten that bad between you and Cindy."

"Hell don't worry about it, you coming over for Sunday's game?" Larry asked casually.

"Yep I'll bring the beer as always."

"Here ya go, chicken, mashed potatoes and corn for you officer and your burger and fries sir. Need anything clse?" shc askcd politcly.

"We're good thanks," Larry spoke, still not looking at her. Wow he must really be trying James thought to himself. He knew Larry was kind of a pervert but didn't realize it was that hard for him to not cheat on his wife. After all Cindy was a beautiful woman even though she had two kids she had a remarkable figure and very pleasant to be around.

James had met Larry in the academy and they became good friends. Larry had met Cindy right after they graduated and married shortly thereafter, and then had two girls, Amanda who was two and Julie who was four, both of which were adorable calling him Uncle James. Both men ate in silence for a few minutes before Larry spoke.

"So where'd they assign you first?"

"Vice of course. Get to have some fun with pimps and hookers for a while. Let's see, how the captain put it? Ah yea, 'I need a little seasoning'. Yea that's it. What the hell am I a piece of meat?" James said clearly not amused.

"Hey man everyone's got to start somewhere don't worry you'll get there, it just takes time. Relax, hell you're still young," Larry told him trying to make him see the lighter side of things.

"Yea you're right, it's just I get so pissed off after spending six years on the traffic beat and now it seems like I'm starting all over again. I mean I took all those night classes and then that damn test which nearly drove me insane. And now I'm going to be running down prostitutes; guess I had higher expectations that's all."

"Well it takes time to learn the streets James. It's a whole different set of rules from writing tickets. You watch your ass out there and everyone around you. You never know how fast things will go from bad to worse in a heartbeat. So do me a favor, pay attention and learn; besides it will help you when you make homicide. Look how many times hookers are killed."

"You're right," James conceded.

"You know I am. Now I got to get back to work, places to go, and tickets to write," Larry said as he stood up reaching for his wallet.

"I got it," James said.

"I knew detectives made good money," he said laughing. "Cover your ass out there, see ya Sunday," he finished with a smile.

"I'll be there," James said and headed for the door.

Chapter 4 Family Matters

Sam's lasting regret about the war was seeing all those poor women and children who through no fault of their own had to live through hell. He had done his best to put all that behind him. Was it the war which made him crazy instead of his brain injury? He'd heard about people who changed because of their head injuries. Some becoming violent while others committed suicide. He could identify with them, he felt like a hollow shell of the man he once was, dealing with excruciating migraines, exquisite tremors of pain that radiated throughout his skull. At times simply hoping to take enough pills to pass out and be free from the ever tightening grip of agony in its purest form.

Sam had found it useless to try to explain to people about how he felt. They didn't know and couldn't understand unless they had to deal with something like his injury. After a while he simply stopped trying to make them understand and whenever someone asked him how he was doing he would put on a fake smile and say okay. It was a lie of course most of the time he was hurting and damn it there was nothing they could do to fix it. He didn't want their sympathy, just left the hell alone.

Ever since the accident pain had been part of his life, his closest companion never leaving, never forsaking him. Of course there were times when it abated for a while due to pain pills. Yet in the back of his mind he knew it would return charging back like a bat out of hell as if to punish him for past transgressions.

In the worst of times the relentless agony made him think of doing insane things; angry, hostile, hating the world around him and everything in it. All those normal bastards who lived pain free, enjoying life as they strutted their happy asses down the street. However Sam knew he was better off than some, there were people in far worse condition than him. People who had to rely on wheelchairs or caretakers to help them live any kind of life, inwardly he chastised himself for acting like a total dick-head. He should be grateful for living at all, the doctors told him it was a miracle he wasn't a vegetable let alone walking and talking. He often thought it would have been better to have died than to endure the pain. Yet he was just being selfish, giving himself a worthless pity trip. *Get your shit together* he thought as he looked into the mirror. It always felt so good to take a hot shower; it relaxed his muscles and even helped with the headaches some.

Sam never felt fully clean until he shaved, maybe where he was in the Army or simply a pet peeve he thought as he wiped the mirror with his hand, then grabbed a dry washcloth to wipe it again. Jacquelyn always hated when she saw hand prints all over it. He shaved and then put on his favorite aftershave. He never wore cologne, couldn't stand the way it smelled.

He got dressed and headed out to the psychic's place. Traffic wasn't too bad which was the opposite of what it usually is whenever he was going somewhere. Before long he reached his destination. He sat in his truck for a moment wondering whether or not to get out and go in. He stared at the small white house in a trance like state when he saw someone move a curtain aside and look out.

Guess that's my cue Sam thought as he climbed out of his pickup and closed the truck door and looked back at the window there was no one there. He walked quickly up to the front door before he changed his mind. Sam never liked spiritual mumbo jumbo. He believed in what he could see and touch. That's why these dreams were so troubling to him. How could they lead him to a dead body when they were no such thing as ghosts? Sam wasn't completely ignorant about the paranormal even though he was skeptical. He knew they were things that modern science couldn't explain.

He didn't see a doorbell as he stood on the old wooden porch with flaking white paint. Just as he was about to knock the faded door opened with a light creaking sound of hinges needing oiled.

"I was wonderin' when you were gonna show up again," said an older heavy set lady wearing a white knitted shawl draped on her shoulders and a black dress with roses.

"What do you mean, back again?" Sam asked surprised. How did this woman know him? Was it someone from his past that he didn't remember because of his amnesia?

She saw the confused look on his face. "Sam darling, don't just stand there, come on in and we'll talk inside," she said in a rich warm tone.

"Why not, after you," Sam gestured politely and followed her into her small but cozy home. In the front room sat a round table covered with a solid red velvet tablecloth and a crystal ball on a gold pestle in the middle. A chair sat on each side of the table across from one another and the whole place reeked of incense. Sam went to sit down on the chair nearest the door.

"No no silly, in here," she said in a playful tone leading him deeper into the house which seemed to be closing in around him. Little beads of sweat began forming on his forehead. Everything slowed down as a powerful sense of déjà vie overtook him. He had been here before, but when? Why? His mind was vainly searching for answers that would not come.

"Are you okay?"

"I'm fine. It's just a little hot in here that's all. Let's get on with this," Sam told her impatiently.

"You never were one for pleasantries," she smiled.

"What's your name? You already know mine."

"Marlene. Please sit," she said pointing to a worn brown leather chair sitting across from an old black recliner where she sat down.

"How do you know who I am? And how many times have I come here?"

"Many times," Marlene smiled.

"What for?" He questioned further.

"I take it they've started again, haven't they?" She made more of a statement than a question as she raised an eyebrow. She could tell right away his anger was rising and knew better to play with him. Samuel Stout was not the type of man you wanted to make angry.

"I'm sorry Sam; I didn't mean to upset you, but you have been here before. I was hoping your memory was better."

"What do you mean?"

"You've been here many times before," Marlene replied flatly.

"You had me going there for a minute I was beginning to think you really were a psychic," Sam smiled.

Marlene raised an eyebrow, "oh but I am my dear Sam."

She made him feel weird when she called him, 'dear'. It was creeping him out and evidently she could tell it as well.

"I'm sorry I forgot you don't like to be called dear. Please forgive the habits of an old woman set in her ways."

"It's okay," Sam said lying, he still didn't like it.

"So let's get down to business shall we."

"Don't you need your crystal ball or something?" Sam asked smartly.

"Anyone with half a brain can see you're bothered by something. Besides the last time you were here, you said the dreams had started again. Have they?"

"Yes, but when was the last time I was here? And how many times have I come here?"

"Well, let me see," she said thoughtfully and paused a moment.

"The first time was around eight or nine years ago. You told me about your accident and you were in therapy and having dreams. Kept talking about some woman named Arlene and having dreams about her," she grew quiet.

"What?" Sam demanded feeling sick to his

stomach.

"You told me about having dreams of the, dead," she said barely above a whisper.

"How many times have I come to you?" Sam asked again.

"Like I said many times, I didn't keep count," Marlene answered.

How in the hell could he have been here many times over the past nine years and not remember any of it. Why was the first visit eight and a half years ago exactly the time Arlene's disappearance? Could he really be a killer, or was Arlene's spirit reaching out to him from beyond the grave and that's why he came to this psychic? He never remembered any dream in particular until now.

"Marlene, what did I talk about the first time I came to you?"

"You spoke of your work accident and worrying over the disappearance of your therapist. I know you very well Sam because… my son used to work for Stout Construction and was…" she paused as if trying to find the courage to continue.

"Please I need to know," Sam begged.

Marlene turned her head as tears rolled down her cheeks.

"My only son David, he was….Sam he was under the crane when it collapsed," Marlene dried her eyes.

"My only son," she started to go on, but Sam cut her off mid-sentence.

"What the hell are you talking about old woman? I was the only one hurt that day," he didn't mean to lose his temper, but he couldn't help it.

"Sam please, you and him were best friends," Marlene tried to interject.

"Shut your fucking mouth! Say one more word…" Sam stopped mid-sentence seeing nothing but red; excruciating screams exploded through his mind. He grabbed both sides of his head and groaned as the world spun out of control and everything went black.

"Oh Jesus!" Marlene said out loud as Sam fell onto the worn red carpet, limp and unconscious. She rushed into the kitchen and grabbed a dish towel ran it under cold water and rushed as fast as she could back to Sam and wiped his face, neck and head. Just like before, she wondered whether or not to call 911. He was breathing good, but felt sweaty and clammy. She knew who to call.

Now she felt bad. Maybe she shouldn't have told him, but she thought he was strong enough. Maybe it was the reason he came to her this time; after all it had been ten years now. She would have to worry with that later right now she had to call his father. She grabbed the phone from the end table and dialed the number

"Hello Stout Construction, how may I help you?" came a pleasant female voice.

"I need to speak with Mr. Stout," Marlene said in a shaky voice. "Who's calling?" the receptionist asked.

"Tell him it's Marlene."

"May I ask what it concerns?"

"Just tell him it's me and he'll answer," Marlene said impatiently

"Yes ma'am," the woman said with a proper tone apparently angry at being bypassed.

Damn nosy secretaries, Marlene thought. A husky male voice came on the line.

"Mr. Stout it's happened again," she said doing her best to steady herself.

"Did you tell him anything?"

"No, he just showed up out of the blue like last time," Marlene told him.

"On my way," Mr. Stout said and hung up the phone. What seemed like an eternity passed before she heard a knock at the door?

"Marlene, it's me."

"Come on in, it's unlocked," she said loudly.

Mr. Stout had two younger men with him who Marlene had never seen.

"Frank you and Jim help me carry him to my truck. Jim you drive Sam's truck and follow me back to his house. I'll call Jacquelyn she'll know whether or not we need to take him on to the hospital. Now let's go before he wakes. Marlene I'll be by later tonight," Mr. Stout said as they hurried out with Sam.

"Take care of him," Marlene called after them.

Was he dreaming again? He felt as though he was having an out of body experience, like floating above the ground carried along by a gentle breeze. The surrounding countryside was rolling hills of green grass dotted with patches of yellow daisies. At least this was a pleasant experience or dream or whatever it was he was having.

When he awoke he was in his bed; he had a pounding headache.

"Good morning, babe," Jacquelyn said softly and kissed him on his forehead.

"What time is it?" Sam asked getting his bearing, he felt so disoriented.

"Eight o'clock hun. I got the kids off to school don't worry. You were sleeping so good I didn't want to wake you."

"Ah babe, that's sweet of you. Tell me what did I ever do to deserve someone as awesome as you are?" Sam looked at her and smiled through his pain, which she picked up on.

"Here hun, take this for your headache," she said reaching him one of his migraine pills and a glass of water. He knew it would make him sleepy though and started to protest.

"Take it honey or your headache will just get worse, you know that," she said in her motherly tone.

"I'll call your dad and let him know you'll be in later ok. Now here you go," she watched as he obeyed and took the pill.

"I would stay a little while but I've got to go to work. I'll call you in a little while and check on you okay," she kissed him on the lips. God she always smelled and tasted so great Sam thought. Turning him on was never a problem.

"Now now control yourself young man. No hanky panky when you're sick," she grinned.

"It's a miracle I'm cured," Sam laughed and tried to raise up when the nausea instantly hit him, almost making him throw up and he laid back down quickly.

"See now I told you. Maybe I should call in babe and take the day off?" Jacquelyn looked worried.

"I'm fine, I'll rest a while and if I don't feel better I'll stay home today okay."

"Call me if you need anything," she told him sternly.

"Yes ma'am."

"Now get out of here you're going to be late," Sam said and smacked her butt.

"You're impossible Samuel Stout," she chastised him.

"Only for you dear, only for you," he smiled as she kissed him again, taking her hand and rubbing his chest.

"Love you, see you soon," she said as she turned to leave.

"Be careful, love you too."

Maybe he would take the day off after all it had been a while since he had taken any time off. Lounge around the house and be there for the kids when they get home. He was still thinking about it when he fell back to sleep.

The migraine medicine definitely made him sleep well. It was 2pm before he got up. Jesus he felt like he had slept for days as he lumbered from the bedroom to the kitchen he was starving. "Hmm," he hummed as he looked through fridge. He picked out some sandwich meat and grabbed the mayo. Nothing like a good ham, cheese and mayo sandwich topped off with an ice cold glass of milk.

Sam felt better after eating. The kids were home before he knew. They came through the door and were overjoyed he was home and spend some time with them before Jacquelyn got home.

"Daddy what are we going to do this weekend?" his son asked.

"We'll have to wait and see won't we," Sam told him. "After all it's only Thursday."

"You so silly daddy it's Friday."

Then his little girl chimed in like a little worried parent, "daddy you need to take some time off, you're mixing days up again."

Again he thought. How often did he do this he wondered as the headache started back again?

"Sorry guys you know how grown-ups are, we always forget things. Who are you two anyway?" he looked at them with a confused look.

"It's us daddy your kids remember," his little girl spoke up. Then Sam made another face.

"Oh yeah you're the one who likes tickling." He grabbed her and started tickling her causing her to go into fits of laughing and Sam's son jumped on his back in defense of his sister.

"And just what is going on here?" Jacquelyn said standing behind them with her arms crossed.

Sam stopped tickling his daughter a second and looked back at Jacquelyn "not my fault, they started it. They ganged up on me," Sam said breathing heavy.

"Is that true children?" Jacquelyn asked raising an eyebrow never once cracking a smile.

"No no mommy, daddy started it," she heard in unison.

"Well I guess..." she paused, "I believe...the kids," and then jumped on Sam as well and all three had him down on the floor tickling him. This made him laugh despite his headache.

"Uncle, I'm done, for," Sam let out a fake gasp and fell over playing dead.

The kids wanted to keep going, but Jacquelyn knew Sam had enough and spoke up. "Okay guys, how about some milk and cookies?" Jacquelyn asked, attempting to give Sam a break.

She knew he was still getting over this last spell. She was going to have to talk with Sam's father and figure out what to do about these lapses he was having again. At least they weren't as frequent as they used to be.

"Baby why don't you go and take a shower and relax while the kids have some milk and cookies," Jacquelyn said lovingly.

"You think you can handle these varmints all by yourself?" Sam asked feeling a headache rising fast from all the horseplay.

"We not ver-mits daddy," Cassie said looking up disapprovingly from her cookie.

"Then what are you? I know, you're daddy's little hooligan."

"Daddy."

Sam moved in closer growling playfully. "Well then, what are you?"

Cassie crossed her arms and said sternly, "I'm

mommy's baby and daddy's girl."

"Well then I'll let you off just this once," he smiled as he gave her a big hug and a kiss on her little rosy cheek. Sam's little boy was oblivious to the scene being content with his milk and cookies.

That was the one thing Jacquelyn loved the most about Sam. He was a great father and she would do anything to protect him and the children. After all she knew what she was getting into when she met him. Although it was difficult at times, she stood by him with absolute determination.

"Now off you go mister," Jacquelyn gently reminded Sam.

"Yes ma'am,"

"Don't 'yes ma'am' me mister, I'm not your mother,"

"Thank god," Sam smiled and reached over and gave her a quick kiss and headed for the bathroom. Maybe a hot shower would help rejuvenate him. He had to figure out why he was having these episodes. It was like a curse hanging over him. Memories, dreams, visions; anymore he couldn't tell what was real and what wasn't.

The one thing Sam knew however was that he was going to get to the bottom of it one way or another. Sam's father had a saying, '*Come hell, high water, bleed or blister*; *get it done*' and that was exactly Sam's sentiment.

Somehow this spiritualist woman he

remembered was a key piece to the puzzle; after all she dealt with death on a daily basis. Or maybe the dead were calling out to him because they were denied justice in this world. Damn it; why did it have to be him to right the wrongs. A cold chill went through his body as he heard a disembodied voice say, "You're the only one who can."

Sam stood motionless in front of the bathroom mirror. Was he hearing things now? *Great, just great; I'm losing my F'ing mind.*

"No you're not," the feminine voice spoke again. Sam turned around half expecting to see Jacquelyn, however the door was closed and no one was in there except himself.

He climbed into the shower trying to forget what just happened. The hot water washed away the chills and he relaxed and cleared his mind a minute before thinking what the voice wanted from him.

"Justice," the female voice came again in answer to his thought.

He didn't need to ask any more questions, he knew exactly what the spirits wanted. They held a vendetta from the grave and could not rest until their killers were punished. If I do maybe they'll leave me alone Sam thought as he washed his muscular chest.

After all killing came easy for him back in the war and since the accident he didn't have normal emotions anyway. *I'm probably a fucking sociopath,* he smiled finishing his shower and getting out. The first one would have to be the person who killed the woman he had recently found. How the hell was he going to find him though?

"Easy," a soft voice whispered into his right ear.

"How?" Sam asked under his breath.

"Just do what we tell you," the voice purred.

"Wait a minute, we? You mean there's more than one?" Sam asked surprised.

"Of course, there are."

"Are you the woman from the grave?" he asked in a low voice afraid of being overheard by Jacquelyn. It would scare the hell out of her if she caught him talking to himself.

"No, I'm just a guide sent to help you."

"Sent by whom?"
"One who cares."

Whenever he heard the voice it caused the tiny hairs on the back of his neck to stand up. Yet he had to see this through.

"What's your name?"

"Alana," came a ghostly reply.

Sam started to ask another question when she cut him off.

"She's coming," Alana said and sure enough Jacquelyn was there.

"You okay honey?" She asked walking up behind him wrapping her arms around his waist and giving him a hug.

"I'm fine, why?"

"Nothing, just making sure that's all. You know me I'm a worry wart."

"Yes you are, but you're my worry wart," he said and turned around and kissed her.

"I feel great baby, quit worrying. Actually I was going to run some errands today. Told dad I'd pick up some blueprints for a new job we're bidding on in Cleveland. I might be late so don't wait up." This was a lie of course, but it would buy him enough time to do some investigating. Besides even if she asked his dad, he never discussed business with anyone, not even Sam's mother. He would still have to be careful and cover his tracks as far as the killings went. He had to make sure they had no way to trace anything back to him.

Once he was out of the house and driving down the road he thought all the voices and images were in his head.

"No they're not," came Alana's voice again in his right ear, causing him to swerve a little.

"Damn it."

"Sorry."

"This is going to take some getting used to," Sam muttered apologetically. "Okay where to?"

"3310 North Oaklawn Street."

"Why?"

"That's where she lived."

"How's that going to help me find the killer?" Sam asked in frustration.

"Isn't that what cops do when they investigate a murder, start at the scene of the crime? Left up here," she said drawing Sam's attention back to the road. "Two blocks on the right. It's a white house with black shutters."

"What are we going to do now?" He asked as he pulled into an empty parking spot across from the house so he could have a good view of anyone coming or going.

"Since Miranda was his last victim, serial killers often return to their house to collect mementos and reminisce about their crime." Alana's voice nearing a whisper.

"Why did you lower your voice?"

"He's coming."

"Who's coming?"

"The killer, idiot."

"My my aren't we testy?" Sam teased

"Aren't you scared?"

"Of what?"

"The killer."

"Hell no. I've seen my share of killing back during the war."

"Even so this man is a killer of many women and death comes natural to him," Alana warned sternly.

"Just worry about yourself, I'll be fine."

"Umm, I'm already dead darling," Alana purred sarcastically.

"True," Sam said with a grin causing Alana to laugh which sounded almost musical.

"Glad to see that you have a sense of humor,"

"I try, after all it's not easy on the other side, it gets rather dead,"

Sam couldn't help but laugh at her witty comeback.

"Shhh, he's getting out of the van," Alana said in a low voice.

An unassuming middle aged man with dark hair and a beard wearing a blue waist length jacket, blue jeans, sneakers was closing the door on a white van that put Sam in mind of the ones used by contractors. He knew this man; he'd seen him in the vision that night at the grave site. The man looked up and then down the street causing Sam to duck down to kept from being seen. Sam spied a peek and saw the man heading though the front yard nearing the house.

He hadn't formulated a plan on exactly how he would go about capturing this bastard. His instincts were to simply shoot him. However he couldn't just walk up and do it in a public place, no this would require more finesse. If there was one thing he could count on was his Airborne Ranger training, even though it had been years since he'd been in action, his training endured.

He felt his heart rate rise as adrenaline surged through his veins. He hadn't felt this alive since sneaking behind enemy lines carrying out reconnaissance missions. Sam refocused his mind as he opened his truck door slowly and gently. By the time he walked around the front of the pickup the man had already disappeared into the house. The predator had now become the prey and justice would be done. It made Sam smile thinking what he was going to do to the good-for-nothing low life bastard. In his mind there was nothing worse than a person who hurt women or children. The world was certainly going to be a better place without this sleaze-bucket. Although it was late September and cold outside now that the sun was down Sam's blood ran hot within, raging with a new passion of raw aggression.

Now his training kicked in, he was on automatic as he made his way up to the house. He crouched down by the front door and listened. He could hear the man's footsteps heading towards the rear of the house. He reached up and slowly turned the doorknob and ever so gently and opened the door just wide enough to slide through.

He didn't have any weapons on him other than his belt knife, but he didn't need any his hands were all he needed. Then a thought occurred to him, he hadn't heard Alana's voice since leaving his truck.

"I'm here," her hushed voice spoke into his right ear, causing him to flinch.

"I didn't want to distract you."

"Appreciate it."

"Want me to go see where he's at?" Alana asked.

"Won't do any good, I have to catch him by surprise as he's leaving," Sam whispered softly.

Then he moved to a better ambush place along a wall where the hallway ends. The serial killer knew how to get around without making much sound. It done all Sam could do to hear his carefully placed footsteps. Yet as soon as the killer exited the hallway, he never knew what hit him. Sam's well placed powerful blow with his fist to the base of the killer's skull laid him out cold causing him to fall face down with a soft thud on the dark brown carpet. Sam wasted no time getting him bound and gagged. He went to the door and cracked it open just enough to see if they were anyone outside. Thankfully this time of year they weren't. He left the killer while he got his truck and pulled in front of the house.

After getting the body rolled up; he drug him inside the rolled carpet to the door and checking one more time before dragging him out to the truck and threw him into the bed.

"He's not dead," Alana told Sam as he was driving to an abandon steel mill outside of Columbus.

"I know," Sam acknowledged.

"I'll finish the job at the mill where they'll be no mess to clean up."

"Good thinking, but what are you going to do with the body?"

"Something to ensure the cops never figure out how he died, yet leave them just enough to identify him so they will know who killed Miranda," Sam stated with confidence as he turned into the abandon parking lot of the dilapidated steel mill. He pulled near the massive steel door and got out of the truck hurried over to the tailgate and opened it and pulled on the carpet until it fell out of the bed and onto the hard gravel parking lot. This time he heard the man give a little whimper.

"Must be waking up; you son-of-a-bitch," Sam cursed and kicked the carpet.

"Don't worry I'm not as sadistic as you." Sam said through clenched teeth as he dragged him through the mill. When he got inside he stopped in front of a large thick metal bucket which looked like a giant pitcher suspended by hooks on each side. He unrolled the carpet and sat the killer up. Sam loosened the gag around Carlson's mouth and then walked around behind him. He turned a couple of valves and made a large blue fire start underneath the iron crucible casting an eerie light around them.

"Who the hell are you? And why have you kidnapped me?" The killer seethed in anger.

"Oh you poor innocent thing you," Sam teased, drunk with pure animal aggression.

"Fuck you; you son-of-a-bitch!"

"Ahh now, that's more like it; the real Luis Carlson. The sick twisted bastard who murdered Miranda Emerson and... let me see ten other innocent women as well," Sam spat back.

Carlson's eyes went wild, "so they sent you to get me, huh? I was wondering when they would?" He finished with a hollow sound to his voice.

"No one sent me, at least no real person," Sam whispered the last part to himself.

"Sam don't let this guy play with your mind, he's very cunning. Make one mistake and he'll kill you," Alana's voice came loud and clear snapping him back to himself.

"You're right."

By that time the cauldron was so hot it was radiating an angry searing red hot aura. Sam pulled a pair of tin snips used for cutting metal and walked over in front of his murderous prisoner. He had no intentions of being extra cruel, simply deal justice and be done with it.

He walked over behind Luis and grabbed his bound hands and cleanly cut both the killer's thumbs off. Luis withered in pain and screamed in agony, causing Sam to smile.

"Now you son-of-a-bitch, maybe you've experienced a fraction of the pain you caused to others. Don't worry you'll be in hell where you belong soon," Sam said delighted as he hooked him to the end of a chain handing down from the large iron overhead beam.

"You bastard, you're no better than me," Luis spat vehemently as he was being raised into the air. "If you want me to beg or confess, I will never give anyone the satisfaction," he finished grinding his teeth together in an insane smile.

"Fine by me," Sam said as he moved him over top of the iron kettle. "I'm not looking for your confession. Say hello to your friends in hell," Sam told him as he lowered him into the searing iron kettle. Even before Luis' feet where inside they burst into flame, causing him to scream.

This delighted Sam immensely. "Scream you son-of-a-bitch. Scream in agony. Scream for all those who you made suffer," Sam taunted, just like he had done in the nightmare.

"Don't Sam; don't gloat, just be done with it," Alana shouted over the screaming.

Finally he lowered Luis all the way down into the kettle and the screams died in a few seconds. The chain went limp and he raised it up revealing a glowing red hook heated by the intense heat inside. In that kind of heat Sam knew the killer's remains would be ashes within minutes.

"I'm sorry Alana," Sam said ashamed of his behavior.

"I understand, but please never get consumed with hatred. I know where that leads," Alana spoke tenderly to him.

Chapter 5 Detective Breckenridge

"Captain Harris wants to see you Detective Colburn." The curt male's voice told him over his police radio. He'd no sooner left the dinner and got in his black unmarked cruiser.

"Ten-four, on my way," he radioed back to the dispatcher.

He wondered what this would be about as he wove his way through traffic, this was the first time the captain had ever called him in. He hoped he wasn't in trouble for last Friday's little slipup downtown. Maybe this would be his first big assignment. Then again maybe he'd get his ass chewed off, either way he would find out soon.

Within a few minutes he was back at the

precinct knocking on the captain's door.

"Come in," came his unmistakable husky voice honed by years of yelling at officers. He took a deep breath, opened the door and walked in. When he walked in he saw another detective already seated in front of the captain's desk.

"Come in and have a seat Detective Colburn. This is Detective Breckenridge," Captain Harris noted in a softer tone. Then Colburn could see why. Detective Breckenridge was a gorgeous woman, wavy dark brown hair and a figure to match.

"Good...after...hello Detective Breckenridge," Colburn stammered. God he couldn't believe he was stuttering. He silently scolded himself as he reached out his hand to shake hers hoping his palms wasn't sweaty.

"Nice to meet you Detective Colburn."

"Nice to meet you too," Colburn said smiling and managing more control when he spoke.

"Anytime," the captain cut in.

"Oh sorry sir," both said in unison as they sat down.

"The reason I called you in Detective Colburn is I want you to assist Detective Breckenridge in an ongoing investigation she's working on. She will fill you in on all the details and bring you up to speed about the current events. You will report directly to me; understand?" Captain Harris told him.

"Yes sir," Colburn answered.

"Detective Breckenridge if you wouldn't mind I'd like to have a word alone with Detective Colburn please," Captain Harris spoke in the most pleasant voice Colburn had ever heard him use. Now he knew something was up.

"No problem sir, I'll wait outside," she said excusing herself.

"Colburn the reason I'm putting you on this case is I want to be informed of everything she does. Detective Breckenridge was placed in our department by the mayor and I don't like it. That pompous son-of-a-bitch thinks he can do whatever he wants. Well we will see about that. However Colburn if you fuck up on this assignment your ass is grass and I'll be the lawnmower. Do you understand?"

"Yes sir."

"Anything else Captain?"

"Yea; knock off that lovey dovie bullshit."

"Huh?"

"You heard me Detective."

"Yes sir, no problem sir," Colburn said trying his best to get the hell out of his office and the awkward situation.

Finally his first real case as long as he didn't screw it up and get busted down to the traffic beat or worse, walking the mayor's dog.

"So Captain Harris wants you to keep tabs on me, huh?" Detective Breckenridge said, making more of a statement than a question catching Colburn off guard when he came out of the Captain's office.

He quickly put on his best poker face, "no not at all, he was just telling me not to screw up my first important case, that's all."

"Umm hmm," Breckenridge raised an eyebrow and grinned.

"Anyway I hope you're a fast learner," she said, suddenly sounding stern handing him a thick manila folder.

"Review this tonight and in the meantime lets grab a cup of coffee and I'll go over the major parts of the case."

This diffidently got his attention.

"I know a great little place with the best coffee, not far from here."

"Cool," was all Colburn could spit out.

He was lost in thought already gleaning through the case file that had information about a series of grisly murders of women in Cleveland.

"Don't worry about the file right now. I'll bring you up to speed; let's go."

"No problem," Colburn said closing the file.

"After you," he said as the elevator door opened. She had a great figure to match her beautiful

face with full luscious lips he thought to himself
as she walked into the elevator. She was nearly as tall
as he was with her high heels on, black slacks with a
black jacket and white shirt underneath. He was
completely taken by her.

"Thank you."

As soon as the door closed she began to fill
him in. The reason the mayor sent me here is my
case has taken a very unusual twist."

"How so?"

"The serial killer I've been tracking for the
past five years has been murdered."

"What's so unusual about that, criminals get
killed by criminals all the time," Colburn said.

"Not serial killers," Breckenridge said as the
elevator doors opened to the parking garage. "You'll
see," she continued walking towards her unmarked
cruiser.

"I guess I don't see what the big deal is? We
should be happy that the sick bastard is dead,"
Colburn said confused.

"Well if you want vigilantes doing your job for
you, that's fine by me, but I prefer to do it the old
fashioned way, good old' detective work," she said
sternly.

"I didn't mean it that way," Colburn said
trying to back-track feeling flustered as they got into
her car.

They sat in an uncomfortable silence until they reached the coffee shop called the Java Cup, which looked warm and inviting.

They walked up to the counter, "What can I get for you?" A short young brunette haired woman asked.

"Medium cinnamon dolce latte, please," Breckenridge said pleasantly.

"And what would you like Detective Colburn?" Breckenridge asked him adding his order to hers.

"Oh, uh just a regular black coffee please."

"Nothing in it?" Breckenridge asked.

"Nope, just black, thanks."

"Coming right up," the cashier said smiling.

Meanwhile Colburn looked around the small coffee shop which had two levels with comfortable looking leather chairs surrounding small round tables. There were even couches on the back wall lined with coffee tables and magazines. Once they were seated at a table in the back corner, Breckenridge wasted no time.

"Detective Colburn."

"Please call me James," he always preferred his first name.

"Okay, James, I know this is your first big case, and I also know you're quite capable of holding your own. Although Captain Harris wants you to spy on me and report back to him," Breckenridge paused taking a sip of her latte. He couldn't help fixating on the fullness of her gorgeous lips; god he was going to have to get a girlfriend soon. It had been over a year since he and Cadence broke up.

"Umm James, are you listening?" Apparently she had sat her drink down and had started talking again, about what he had no clue.

"Sorry Detective Breckenridge."

"Call me Sarah."

"Sorry Sarah, I was just wondering why is this so important that the mayor is involved."

"Don't you understand James, if it gets out that a serial killer was murdered by a vigilante and it was kept secret; the press will have a field day with it."

"Oh," James said raising an eyebrow. "First of all, how do you know he was killed by someone wanting revenge?"

"His remains were found just outside the eighteenth precinct's front door, well what little was left of him anyway," Sarah said grimly.

"What do you mean by; 'what little was left of him'?"

"A pile of ashes was found by an officer at 6:30am yesterday morning on his way out."

"That doesn't mean that it was a person's ashes, could be anything, and how can you identify someone by that?" James asked clearly getting more confused by the minute.

"We wouldn't have been able to, except that there was a severed thumb along with a typed written letter placed on top of the pile of ashes. There's photos in the case file and also a copy of the letter, which tells us that we should be thanking him for doing our job. It also contains the location where the last victim is buried; forensics is still out there combing the area to see if there are any other victims."

"How do you know it's a man?"

"We don't."

"Man this is right out of some sick twisted movie," James said in a mixture of amazement and confusion.

"I see why this can't get out until we can get a handle on it. I've never heard of anything like this, it's certainly bizarre."

"We used the print off the thumb and it confirmed the identity of one, Louis Michael Carlson. Who had two arrests, one for petty larceny a year ago and indecent exposure three years ago."

"Has the ashes been analyzed to see if they are human?"

"Lab results came this morning and based on composition and weight."

"Weight?"

"Yes, you can tell the approximate size of a person based on the weight of the ashes, assuming that we have all of the ashes, it would be around his size. Also the chemical ratio of carbon and other chemicals which make up the human body."

"Interesting, but how do you know Carlson was a serial killer?" James asked still trying to get his head around everything.

"Four years ago there were a series of murders in Cleveland, we recovered five bodies. There may be more, but we ran into a dead end. I was called up there to assist a special unit on the case; he came up as a suspect in the slaying of Sandra Collins. We never had enough evidence to charge him with anything."

"So why did you continue to investigate him?" James asked.

"Call it a gut feeling, I knew that slimy bastard was guilty."

"Oh my, what a potty mouth we have," James said teasingly.

Sarah looked at him sarcastically, "I'm a detective shit for brains, you know any who don't cuss?"

"My bad, just took me by surprise, that's all."

She could tell he meant no harm, "I'm sorry James, it just pisses me off that someone thinks they can be; judge, jury, and executioner," she said getting back onto the topic at hand.

"I can tell," James agreed, glad to be past the awkward moment.

"So what's our game plan?" James asked earnestly.

"Since Carlson was cremated, I'm having all the funeral homes with crematories checked; maybe the killer works at one. And I have a search warrant for where he lived."

"You mean he lives here? How did you know?" James asked surprised.

"After Cleveland his trail went cold, it wasn't until another victim turned up last year here in Columbus that we knew he had changed cities. Again this one fit the others exactly." Sarah said pulling out a paper from her satchel.

"Take a look at this," she said as she handed it over to him.

The paper had a pentagram drawn on it facing to the north and an X at each point overlaid on the city of Cleveland, with the distance of five miles between each point.

"So we're dealing with a Satanist?" James asked not understanding what she was showing him.

"At first we thought we were, however a Satanist pentagram is turned to where the two points that form the bottom are at the north end. When the first victim turned up it was at the area marked on the map; the second one was found five miles thirty-six degrees southwest of the first one, the third was exactly five miles found thirty-six degrees northeast and as you can guess victims four and five completed the pentagram. And now it has started again in Columbus. We can use the pattern to determine where the other possible victims are buried." She continued seeing she had James' complete attention, "also each victim was killed differently."

"Then what's his M.O.?" he asked getting even more interested.

"At first we were puzzled by the different ways we found the bodies and how each was killed. In the beginning we thought we were only dealing with one person. Yet once we began to put all the pieces together, it pointed to it being a possibility of five serial killers working together; we called the group the Alchemists. That's why although the victims' deaths were different. Each had been murdered in a way that deals with the five elements. Now it's happening all over again."

"Five, I thought they were four; earth, fire, water, and air?"

"You're right James, but many consider spirit to be the fifth element and the most mysterious. Each one had the corresponding mark on top of them where they were buried that indicated the element used to kill them. For example we had bodies in Cleveland that were drown, crushed by earth, suffocated, and found cremated remains. As far as the spirit method of killing we were unable to confirm a cause of death," Sarah replied.

"Was you able to link any of the murders to Carlson or others?" James said scratching his head.

"Unfortunately they were very good at covering their tracks leaving behind no fingerprints or DNA. There was nothing to tie Carlson or any of his associates, if he had any, to the bodies we recovered. We managed to keep it out of the press and identify most of the victims. This time we will catch those responsible before they disappear and start in another city."

James was inwardly cursing that something like this was dumped on him for his first big case; at least his new partner was attractive.

"Do you think it's the same group operating here now? Could it be a branch or do you think they have more than five members?" James ask.

"I think they may be more than one group, but we won't know until we get more information about the one here. If the killings stop after our suspect kills the fifth person representing the spirit element then we'll know there was one group. Once you go over the files tonight you'll have a better understanding of the case. Now we have to go and execute a search warrant where Carlson was living," Sarah said and then took a long drink from her latte.

"How do you know he lived here?" James asked.

"I was closing in on him after I saw a report of an attempted abduction of a woman who fit the victims profile, young, twenty to twenty-five, black hair, slim build. After interviewing her and getting a description I knew it was him and now was my chance. Well it would have been, had it not been for this damn vigilante who got to him first. Anyway we canvassed the neighborhood and had him under surveillance, when he simply disappeared," Sarah said flustered.

Now James could really see why she was so angry, over five years of detective work down the drain and no answers for the families.

"What makes you think you found his house?" James asked.

"We have a witness that puts him going into a house on the north end of town, near Worthington off Old Wilson Creek Road, that's where were heading from here."

"Sounds like a fun evening," James said lightly, trying to ease the ominous mood that filled the air.

"What do you think we'll find?" James asked on their way out of the coffee shop.

"Not really sure, most serial killers have a perfectly normal house as a front so we'll have to be on the lookout for trapdoors, fake walls, or any signs that lead to a secret chamber somewhere."

"And you're sure about this guy?"

"Positive, I've spent the last five years on this case and everything points to him. He may be the ring leader, going to different cities recruiting others to join him. "

Now James understood her anger even more, that not only had someone got even, but wiped out all her work.

"So it's not just about someone being a vigilante?" James spoke the words before he thought. Damn it now he was in for it, he could see the anger rising in her face.

"Listen smartass, I don't like vigilantes or the fact that this one fucked up years of detective work."

"Ease up crack head, I didn't mean anything by it, we're both on the same side remember?"

"James, did you just call me a crack head?" Sarah asked pointy.

He felt his anger die the instant he looked at her beautiful face, "sorry."

"Sorry is right James! I was a crack addict for over five years before getting clean," Sarah said flatly without a hint of emotion to her voice.

Oh shit he really fucked up now, "Sarah, I'm really sorry, I… why are you laughing?"

"I'm fucking with you; I had to get even, besides you're so gullible," she said sweetly and smiled with a wink.

Was she flirting with him? God he hoped so, but he better play it cool he told himself as they got into her cruiser.

The ride over was spent in silence as both were lost in thought; before long they were pulling up in front of a nondescript house.

"This is it, don't let your guard down in there," Sarah said getting out.

"What do you mean, he's dead?"

"All we have is his thumb and some ashes that could be anyone's."

"You think he's sick enough to cut off his own thumb to make us think he's dead? Did he know you were getting close?"

"Possible, just be careful," she said as her weapon came sliding out of her holster.

She saw James eyeing her pistol, "9mm Beretta, custom pearl hand grips, nickel finish, it even has a special magazine that holds seventeen and one in the chamber," she said.

"Well now you're just making me feel inadequate," James smiled as he pulled his gun.

"What are you talking about? You're packing a 45 caliber Sig Sauer Titanium Edition."

"Damn girl I'm beginning to like you more and more."

"You want the front or back," she asked as

they approached the house.

"Your call."

"I'll take the back, just don't get carried away and shoot me inside," she said with a smirk.

"As soon as you hear me yell at the front door, go in," James told her. With a nod she headed around to the back of the house, pistol raised. He gave her enough time as he positioned himself in front of the door.

"POLICE, OPEN THE DOOR!" He yelled and kicked the door open. He didn't figure anyone would be there, but better go by the book. Nothing moved or was out of the ordinary as he made his way through the living room which was impeccably clean. However there was a faint smell of musk mingled with decay; whatever it was it made his jaw clench tight.

He raised his gun and stepped near a closed door off to the left; slowly he reached down and turned the knob slowly. The door creaked as he slowly opened it with his weapon first he entered the room. It was laid out with Victorian style furniture; again impeccably clean with a thin layer of dust and that same smell, it made his skin crawl.

Suddenly a shadow caught the corner of his eye from the corner of the room. In a flash he whirled around, and saw nothing but a door to what appeared to be a closet. A creaking sound from behind him caused him to do a one-eighty, white knuckling his gun prepared to fire in a split second.

"IT'S ME!" Sarah yelled.

He lowered his weapon.

"Sorry Sarah, just something about this place that's all."

"I know, same here."

"You find anything?"

"Nothing; you?"

"When I was checking the room I thought I saw a shadow over there near the closet and was going over to check it out when you showed up. Probably just the light coming through the curtains was all," James told her.

"Might as well check it out too; let's see what's in there."

"Okay," James said taking a step toward the closet door.

He looked at Sarah, "On three, one; two; three." He opened the door fast and Sarah was there weapon poised to fire on any threat, however it was just a regular closet with clothes hanging and shoes on the floor.

"Guy's certainly a neat freak," Sarah said as she stepped into the closet for a closer look.

"James; look."

"Where?"

"Here in the back left corner."

"I don't see anything," no sooner than the words left his mouth, Sarah stepped forward placed her hand a narrow floor board. A soft whooshing sound caused both of them to step back repositioning their guns.

"Figured," Sarah said in a low tone.

"Figured what?" James asked still stunned at the discovery. Was this where the shadow was trying to lead him?

"Sick bastard has his own little horror chamber right off his bedroom," Sarah said in disgust.

This diffidently wasn't like busting hookers James thought to himself, developing an uneasy feeling in the pit of his stomach. The kind he got whenever he was going to face something which was going to be extremely unpleasant.

"Here let me go in first," he said taking a step toward the secret passageway.

"Me first, remember it's my case. Watch my back."

"Sarah," James protested in vain as she vanished from sight. "Damn it," he muttered going in after her.

It took a few seconds for his eyes to adjust to the darkness. He couldn't see her or hardly anything else, when suddenly a light flickered on in front of him blinding him for a few seconds.

"All clear."

"That's good because I can't see shit, you blinded me with the damn light."

"Sorry about that, I stumbled across the light switch and didn't want to waste the element of surprise."

"Well you didn't," he smirked, and then smiled; before they could say anything else their surroundings made their jaws drop.

"Wow!" James exclaimed.

"I've never seen anything like this," Sarah said equally stunned by the ghoulish scene before them. Directly in front of them was an alter bathed in blood with a red; white, and black candle sitting on each side of a human skull which had a red candle on top of it. The candles had been burned many times and melted wax had streamed down the sides adding to the gruesome scene.

"This guy was a sick son-of-a-bitch," James said in disgust. He had seen enough horror flicks to know this had to do with voodoo or some type of witchcraft at least.

"What do you make of it?" James asked her.

"The altar has the elements of voodoo, however the markings on it and look at the floor here," she said pointing.

They put their latex gloves on before moving closer to study things. The altar and floor were made of the same stone blocks and were carved all over with various types of symbols.

"Is that paint?" James asked running his finger along a snakelike symbol.

"No, it's blood," she said examining it closer.

"Man this guy is one sadistic son-of-a-bitch," James repeated his earlier statement.

"That's for sure; there are many voodoo signs here, but I'm not sure what these are," Sarah said pointing to the left side of the altar.

"Looks like he's mixing voodoo with occult black magic see the inverted pentagram in the circle."

"How do know so much about this stuff?" James asked her.

"I'm a witch James," Sarah said in a serious tone.

"You're full of shit."

"Really? Careful or I'll curse your ass."

"Sorry," James said meekly and laughed, and then quickly asked to be sure. "Are you?"

"No James," Sarah laughed.

He could tell this was going to be a great partnership, the chemistry was there, he wondered if she felt that same way.

"I studied anthropology and religion in college," she said answering his question from earlier.

"Look at this sign, it's a voodoo sign for one of their spirits, yet this one is an ancient Sumerian symbol for their god of the dead," she said pointing to the one on the left side of the altar.

This gave him the creeps, he never considered himself a superstitious man, but he had only seen stuff like this in the movies. He had been raised in a Baptist home and deep down believed in God and devil as well, which he had certainly seen enough of.

"We better call forensics in," Sarah said as she moved toward the left wall. "Hmm," she mumbled.

"What?"

She was standing over two large symbols in the floor, "these are symbols for earth and fire."

"So?" James asked confused.

"So; that deals with alchemy and means Carlson was dealing with at least three different elements in his deranged killing spree. At one time alchemy was considered magic and even banned under penalty of death. And look on the right side of the room; they are symbols for air and water."

"What is the symbol in the center of the room?" James asked feeling himself being drawn into the whole mystery.

"I'm not sure," Sarah replied.

"This place just gets creepier and creepier," James said looking over her shoulder at the floor. "I'll call our forensics team," he said pulling out his cell phone.

"That's strange."
"What is?" Sarah asked.

"No signal."

"Mine either," Sarah said with a puzzled look.

"He's probably sealed this chamber in some way to prevent them from working," James said searching for a signal.

"Let's try upstairs," James suggested, hoping to get the hell out of the basement chamber.

"What's wrong?" he asked noticing Sarah was being unusually silent.

"Louis Carlson wasn't your average serial killer, James."

"Sarah is there anything average about anyone who kills? Come on let's get out of this damn place, it gives me the creeps," James told her.

As soon as they were back upstairs she was on the phone, however it wasn't forensics.

"That's right, you heard me…exactly. We're dealing with something far worse than I thought," Sarah said into the phone, with who James had no idea.

"You call in forensics?" he asked.

"No."

"Then who was that?"

"The mayor."

"I don't understand?"

"I'll fill you in later, I've got to go."

"Is there something you're not telling me?" James asked both concerned and confused.

"James I promise I'll fill you in later, but right now I have to go."

"Go where?"

"Wait here until forensics gets here and make sure you get a full report, and catch a ride back to headquarters with them. I'll call you later tonight."

"Yes ma'am you're in charge," James said angered that he was being left out.

"Damn it James I don't have time for childish games. I need you here; it's important that this place be gone over with a fine tooth comb. I don't want anything missed, so be damn sure it doesn't. Besides since I can't be here you're the next best thing."

"Just remember I'm a rookie detective."

"Bullshit, you may be new at being a detective; however I've done my homework. Why do you think you were assigned to me? Now I really have to go, unless you want to argue some more?"

"You mean it wasn't Captain Harris' decision?" James asked stunned.

"Hell no! He wanted Detective Maddox. Harris wanted someone he knew he could trust to spy on me. He hates any interference in his department, plus he and the mayor have a history."

"Oh, I'm sorry Sarah," he said feeling like an idiot.

"Just make sure they tear this house apart."

"No problem."

"Also I'm having special equipment called ground penetrating radar bought out, in case my suspicious prove correct."

James knew what that equipment done, "You think he buried people in the backyard?"

"Maybe, we need to be through, at this point we have to make sure we cover all angles. If he had a partner he may have killed him to cover his tracks and then started killing again. If Carlson acted alone, someone found out what he was doing and killed him, either way we got to get to the bottom of this."

James still didn't like the idea of not going with her.

"Look, I'll call you when I'm done and we'll go over everything. I know Captain Harris is up your ass, but do me a favor and don't piss him off. We're walking a fine line with this case and we damn sure don't need any screw ups." Sarah told him bluntly.

"No problem," Colburn said as she left.

Not long after the forensics team showed up, for which he was glad, he was anxious to get the hell away from the creepy ass house. Finally they had photographed; cataloged, bagged, and tagged all the evidence from the scene. The sweeps of the property with the ground penetrating radar didn't reveal anything.

<u>Chapter 6 The Day After</u>

"Thanks Richard for meeting me on such short notice. We can talk here the kids are at the sitters," Jacquelyn said warmly.

"Has he had any more episodes you're aware of?" Richard asked deeply concerned.

"No."

"Do you think we need him see the neurologist again?"

"Not yet, his checkup is next month, let's see if we can wait. I don't want him getting worried. You know what stress does to him."

"Okay, but if he has another spell like this past one, we'll take him right away."

"Of course."

"Does he remember anything?" Richard asked. She could see the buried pain from the past coming back to haunt him.

"No Richard and we will see to it that he never will. It would kill him to know," she said placing her hand on his shoulder.

"If he would just stay away from that damn old gypsy," Richard said through clenched teeth.

"You know she loves Sam like a son, even though she lost her son in the accident she would never hurt him."

"Sorry, I know, but if she slips and tells him about her son or… he's strong, but he wouldn't be able to handle it."

"Don't worry we will keep that from happening."

"Sorry, but she also knows about…"

"Richard I told you to quit worrying," she cut him off before he could speak Sam sister's name. "The doctor told us that Sam's memory loss is permanent as long as he takes his medicine he should be find."

"Let's hope so," Richard said sounding less than optimistic.

"If we over react he will pick up on it and won't stop until he finds out why. You know how he is," Jacquelyn said firmly.

"You're right."

"I'll let you know if anything happens, but it's time for me to go and pick up the kids. Are you going to be able to come over for dinner tomorrow?"

"Wouldn't miss it, six?"

"Yes."

"See you then," he said standing up.

She let him out and grabbed her keys and cell phone and left to get the kids. Sam still wasn't back by the time she had the kids in bed. She always worried about him. It was no good to try and call him; he only kept a cell phone in the glove box in case of emergencies. Which was probably good seeing how he would wreck if he tried to use it while driving, he wasn't the most tech savvy man. And on top of that, his brain injury made it difficult enough to drive. So she resigned herself to a long bath and then went to bed. Sometime in the middle of the night she felt him trying to get into bed without waking her.

"Hey babe," she said sleepily.

"Sorry I woke you honey," Sam said softly.

"It's okay," she said rolling over to face him.

"Umm you smell good," Jacquelyn said snuggling closer to him.

"Just showered, long day and I needed one," he smiled.

She took his cheeks into her hands and pulled him close and kissed him passionately. He may have his problems, but not in the bedroom she thought as she gave into the passion.

"You're smiling an awful lot this morning, what's the occasion?" Jacquelyn asked.

"I always smile the day after I get lucky," Sam laughed and smacked her butt lightly.

"Keep that up and we'll have a repeat," she grinned seductively.

"Promise," Sam winked.

Of course that wasn't the only reason he was in such a great mood, though they were so many questions running through his mind it was impossible to keep track of them. The main question was he really a sociopath to have no emotion or a psychopath because of the rage and satisfaction he felt over killing Louis Carlson? It ignited an incredible desire within him to find even more evil people to kill. Why him? Why out of all men was he chosen?

"Sam, my dear Sam," Alana's voice purred in his ear, "what's troubling you?"

"Why me?" he asked barely above a whisper.

"What babe?" Jacquelyn asked entering the room unseen by Sam.

"Nothing, just talking to myself," he answered trying to sound light hearted.

"As long as you don't go answering yourself, you're okay," she smiled and kissed him on his forehead.

"Why don't you rest today babe while I take the kids over to see your parents. They've wanted to have them over; you know how much they love spoiling them," Jacquelyn suggested.

"Actually that sounds good, I'm a little bit tired from the trip to Cleveland," Sam lied; he wanted to have some time alone with Alana. He had to get answers if this was the path his life was going to take, so be it, as long as he knew why.

No sooner than Jacquelyn and the kids had left Alana spoke, "Sam you must trust me, the answers will come when the time is ready," she spoke in a warm compassionate tone.

"Am I just supposed to go on faith?" Sam asked

"Ask yourself; how do you feel about killing Carlson?" Alana asked.

"I don't know, how am I supposed to feel?" Sam said bluntly.

"You saw his victims; you know what a monster he was."

"I know he deserved what he got, but is it my place to be; judge, jury, and executioner?"

"You're the only one who can; you're the only one who can see them, and the truth. Isn't that enough?

"For now," Sam said as he ground his teeth, "for now."

"Why haven't I seen you Alana?" Sam asked changing the subject.

"Because you haven't asked too," she spoke softly with a slight musical tone, delighted he wanted to see her.

"Well?"

"Well, what?" she teased.

"Show yourself," Sam said quickly.

"Aren't we bossy?" Alana sassed back.

Suddenly a ghostly image of a beautiful dark haired young woman appeared, she was young with bright green eyes, incredibly life like.

"I can only imagine how beautiful you were in real life," Sam said stunned by her glorious form.

Alana's face turned from a ghostly white to a pale rosy color.

"Why Alana are you blushing?" Sam asked, noticing the color change.

"No why?" Alana asked in a nervous tone before her beautiful shape shimmered and went out.

"Hey, where'd you go?" Sam asked.

Silence was his only answer, he wondered if

he embarrassed her. How can you embarrass a ghost he thought. Well they still have feelings, maybe she's bashful.

"I'm here," she said barely above a whisper. "It takes a lot of energy to manifest myself," Alana explained as her voice grew stronger.

"I'm sorry I didn't know, I thought… never mind."

"What?" Alana purred.

"I thought maybe I embarrassed you or something. It looked like you were blushing," Sam explained.

"It's been a long time since a man has paid me a compliment, you reminded me of someone I knew long ago; besides spirits can't blush darling," Alana purred in her sultry seductive tone.

God Sam thought, I must be crazy I get along with dead spirits better than I do with the living.

"You're not crazy Sam, just very special. You've been to the other side and it marked you and that mark is visible to us," Alana said.

"But, why now; it's been ten years?"

"Because now you seek the answers that have been hidden from you and you are strong enough to do what is needed," Alana told him.

"If I ever find out what it is?" Sam said feeling frustrated.

"Soon my darling Sam, soon."

"So you say."

"So I promise," Alana said as her smiling face reappeared. "Sam darling I want you to trust me and know we are doing the right thing."

He decided to come clean and tell her, "Alana since my accident I don't have the right emotions."

"What do you mean?" Alana asked already knowing the answer.

"I don't feel things the way normal people do," he was doing a terrible job of explaining it.

"I know you don't, if you were like other people I wouldn't have come to you," Alana said trying to encourage him.

"Sam when you had your accident and died before they brought you back, your spirit traveled into our realm," Alana explained.

"Is that why I'm different?"

"Yes that experience changed you forever."

Sam nodded in silent agreement.

"You have been given a gift from on High."

"On High?"

"The Almighty God," she clarified.

"Really?" Sam asked in awe.

"Yes Sam, after all I have no reason to lie to you. I am not of this world so its corruption does not affect me," she said and then continued. "Patience my darling, patience; very soon everything will become clear." She placed her ghostly pale hand on the left side of his face. He felt a cold tingling sensation on his cheek.

"I promise," Alana spoke solemnly.

"I trust you," Sam spoke barely above a whisper putting his hand to his cheek as if to touch hers and felt his cool skin beneath.

"I forget you're a spirit sometimes," he said lowering his hand.

"It's okay," Alana said softly. She could sense a deepening bond growing between them.

"So now," she spoke with a lighter tone, "we must plan for the next one."

"The next one?" he asked coming back out of his thoughts.

"Yes, Louis Carlson wasn't the only one. There are others like him dealing in the same things he did. The killings will not stop until they are dealt with," Alana said.

"How many are they?" Sam asked tensely.

"They are four more, even more dangerous than Louis."

"What does all this mean?" He asked deep in

thought about the meaning behind the killings and what they had in common.

"At this point I don't know everything, however things will become clearer as we keep uncovering the truth by tracking down the others. I know the five share the same motives and driven by the same goal."

"What insane motives would five men have in common for them to be murdering innocent women?"

"That's why the Nabila summoned me to come to aid you in stopping them."

"Nabila?" Sam asked confused.

"A Nabila is what some may refer to as a gypsy queen, however they are much more than that. They are descendants of an ancient line of Sumerian Priestess. There is only one per generation at a time on earth and they are the only one powerful enough to summon me."

"When was the last time you were summoned?"

"It's been many years ago my darling," Alana purred.

"Why?" Sam asked, his curiosity getting the best of him.

"Oh they were several reasons, but that's not important now. However," she continued, "this time it is to avenge the blood of the innocent through a willing vessel and stop the terror about to unfold."

"What's a vessel?" Sam asked raising an eyebrow.

"My dear Sam, she purred in her seductively sweet voice, "one who brings justice to those who have been denied. The time has come for the Cleansing, finally the cries of the innocent have been heard and now vengeance is loosed upon the wicked."

"We'll see," Sam said lightly.

"Sam you are so much more than you know," Alana said reassuringly.

"You keep saying that."

"And I'll keep saying it until you believe it," Alana smiled.

Sam smiled, "if you say so."

"I do."

Suddenly a blurred image flashed through Sam's mind of an oddly familiar young woman.

Alana noticed Sam's distant look, "What's wrong my dear Sam?"

"Nothing."

But she could tell something had disturbed him.

"Darling what was it?" Alana asked again, her voice filled with compassion.

"An image of a young woman I think I knew her, yet…" Sam quit speaking, trying hard to remember the face now hidden, gone into the depths of his damaged mind.

That told Alana what she needed to know, he was beginning to remember.

"Don't worry I'm sure it will come back to you," Alana said encouragingly.

Chapter 7 The Leak

"So what's the word from the mayor?" James asked as he walked up to outside the coffee shop where they had met earlier in the day.

"Let's talk inside over a hot cup of coffee," Sarah told him as she opened to the door. It was late and the shop was deserted except for the barista. Perfect she thought a chance to relax and go over everything with James.

They got their coffee and went and sat at the back corner booth so they could be out of earshot of anyone who may come in.

"Well apparently someone from the eighteenth precinct leaked the story to the Columbus Reader and it's going to be front page news first thing in the morning edition. The mayor is going to have the chief of police hold a press conference first thing in the morning to try and contain the story and start damage control. God knows the press is going to have a field day with it," she finished.

"Oh shit," James said grimly.

"Yeah," she agreed.

"Damn Captain Harris is going to be furious and up my ass eight ways to Sunday."

"Well on the bright side at least we have a heads up and won't be caught with our pants down," Sarah said attempting a smile.

"Oh you perv."

"What?" James asked innocently.

"I saw that grin," she smirked at him.

"Don't know what you're talking about," he lied with a big smile.

"Umm hmm," she smiled.

"Anyway we have our work cut out for us, the mayor wants us to brief the chief of police at 7am in the morning before the press conference at 8am," Sarah was saying before James' phone rang interrupting her.

"Fuck, its Harris," James grimaced.

"Hello sir; yes sir; no sir…" was all he could say before Harris hung up on him.

"I take it, he found out about the leak?"

"Hell yes and he's pissed."

"Can't blame him."

"Yeah, but why me?" James asked gravely.

"Because you're special," Sarah said with a wink and a smile doing her best to lighten his mood.

"Yeah boy," James managed a weak attempt at a smile. He knew she was being supportive.

"Now where were we?" James asked trying to get back on the topic of the day's events. He'd better be prepared for the captain's interrogation tomorrow morning. So he gave her a rundown of what the forensics team found.

"So nothing in the yard?" She asked.

"Nope."

"Okay," she nodded.

"What about the location mentioned in the letter, anything there?"

"Yes, a body was there and the preliminary report says that it is a female Caucasian, mid-twenties, no obvious cause of death. The medical examiner will have to do a full autopsy, which we'll have the results in tomorrow evening. We are treating it as a homicide. The victim still had her pocketbook which contained her ID and credit cards, so it wasn't robbery. According to her ID her name was Miranda L. Emerson and assuming her address is correct she lived at 3310 North Oaklawn Street close to the campus. She was reported missing six months ago by her parents; that's how we got their address."

"Have you sent anyone out to her parent's house at 101 N. Maple Ave?"

"Uniforms are there now waiting on us. After we go by there we will check her house near campus," she told James.

"What are we waiting for?"

"Let's go, you drive, I need to think."

"Yes ma'am," James said curtly.

Sarah rolled her eyes and smiled.

James laughed as they headed to his unmarked cruiser. Sarah was silent the whole way there. He left her alone; he knew the value of quiet time.

He saw the patrol car as he pulled onto the street sitting in front of the house, slowly he pulled in behind.

"Why don't they have their lights on?" James asked still thinking like a uniformed officer that he'd been.

"No reason to alarm the neighbors besides, this is Miranda's parents home," Sarah said dismissively coming out of her thoughts.

They got out and walked up to the patrol car and she knocked on the window, with that both officers got out.

"Evening detectives," Sergeant Smith who was

the senior officer of the two spoke.

"Evening," James and Sarah said in unison.

"Let's see what we can find out," Sarah said turning toward the house.

"We've been here for the last thirty minutes and haven't seen any activity, there's a light on inside the house and a red Chevy Lumina car in the driveway. It's registered to a; he paused to look at his notebook, Susan Emerson," Sergeant Smith finished.

"Must be family, possibly her mother who also filed a missing person's report," Breckenridge informed them as they all headed to the front door. After this we will go over to Miranda's house.

Sarah rang the doorbell; the moment they stood waiting seemed like an eternity to James. The door finally opened.

"Hello," said a middle-aged woman with long black hair.

"Hello, my name is Detective Breckenridge and we are here to see if you are the mother of Miranda Emerson."

The color drained from the woman's face at the realization of what the visit was about.

"I'm Mrs. Emerson, Miranda's my daughter, please come in," she said leading them into the living room.

"Please sit," Mrs. Emerson said pointing to the

nearby couch.

"I'm so sorry to have to tell you, we may have found your daughter and need you to help us with identifying her. It would speed the process up if we have something of hers that contained her DNA, like a hair brush perhaps? We found a pocketbook with her id as part of her belongings, however to make sure we need to match her DNA," Sarah said gently.

Mrs. Emerson sat there quietly as tears streamed down her face.

"Could you provide us with something?"

"Yes of course," Mrs. Emerson said somberly getting up and going into one of the back rooms returning with a hair brush. This was hers she would come over sometimes after going to the gym to shower.

"Will this work?" she asked reaching it to Sarah.

She took it by the handle and saw a few strands of hair, "yes this will work fine. Officer Smith will you get this to the medical examiner ASAP," Sarah said as she produced a small plastic evidence bag from an inside pocket of her coat.

"Yes ma'am, anything else Detective Breckenridge?" Sergeant Smith asked walking to get the bag containing the brush.

"That's all for now sergeant, thanks," Sarah said politely. And with that the two patrolmen left.

She went on with the standard line of questioning; finally reassuring Mrs. Emerson she would find the one responsible and making arrangement to contact her as soon as the DNA results were in.

"Okay off to Miranda's house," Sarah told James as they left.

"No problem,"

It was a short drive to Miranda's place.

"James go ahead and call for CSU to come out and go over this place while we give it a once over."

"Sure thing."

They crossed the street and walked up to the front door and knocked to check to see if anyone was there before they entered. A search of the house revealed nothing at first.

"James look at the way the floor is cleaner in this area in the front living room."

"You're right, there's a neat oval shape where there is no dust. Do you thing that someone used it to wrap up a body?"

"Very likely that Carlson may have kidnapped Miranda in her own home."

"But wasn't this place searched when the missing person's report was filed six months ago." "It should have been; we'll get the report first thing in the morning. Maybe something in it will help us find the link between Carlson and Miranda, which in turn will lead us the right way."

"I'll get right on that first thing," James said.

"Listen James I'm beat, let's get some rest and meet in the morning after the press conference," Sarah told him as they got into his car.

"Sounds good to me, hopefully Captain Harris won't throw me back on traffic after this," James said thinking of the ass chewing he was going to get in the morning.

"Don't worry I have a feeling it won't be so bad," she said calmly.

"Hope you're right," James said trying to sound upbeat.

After that, the rest of the ride back to the precinct was quiet, each one absorbing the day's events.

With a quick goodbye she got into her unmarked patrol car and sped off into the night.

Chapter 8 Flickering Flames

Sam gazed into the flickering flame of the candle sitting on the table in front of him. It was calming to watch the single flame dance, gently waving from side to side; the soft warm glow instilled an inner peace. When he shifted his eyes out of focus he could draw little rays of light and look into them watching tiny particles floating through the air.

Doctors told him his occipital lobe of his brain had been damaged and that was the reason his vision changed. So he never brought it up, after all it was something he enjoyed.

No one understood him, no one knew what he'd been through, and no one knew his pain. Sometimes he wished he had someone he could talk who wouldn't get upset or judge him. Maybe that's why he liked Alana so well, yet she could be a figment of his imagination.

"No Sam darling I'm real," Alana appeared on his right side.

"I'm glad you are," Sam said, his mood improved anytime she was around.

"Where have you been? You've been gone all day."

"I'm sorry darling, next time I'll tell you when I have to go. I didn't mean to worry you," she said tenderly.

"It's okay, it's just when you're not around I think I must be losing my mind and start thinking you're not real and I made you up. Besides with Jacquelyn working all day I was lonesome. "

He felt a tingling sensation in the middle of his right cheek causing him to turn and see Alana moving slowly away.

"There, how was that for real? See you felt that on your cheek when I kissed you just now," Alana purred.

"That was…you; how?" Sam stuttered, surprised again by the ghostly contact. "How?" he repeated.

"Because you believe and are chosen," Alana said smiling.

That reinforced the realness of her to him. It was one thing to see or hear something, but to feel it was a whole other story. He trusted his instincts, believing it was the only thing that kept him alive during the war and now it was telling him this was real.

"The reason behind my absence today darling; I located another one," she said getting back on topic.

"Another one," Sam said coming back out of his thoughts. "What's his name?"

"Alexander Demarkov, he is one of the Avox."

"Did you say, Avox?" Sam asked not sure he heard her right.

"Yes, it is a group of five men who takes the Akashic Oath in a bid for everlasting life."

Sam knew what an oath was, "what does Akashic mean; and why all the killing; are they Satanist?"

"The Avox has roots tracing back to alchemy when its practitioners tried to unlock the secrets of the spirit element. They began adopting voodoo religious rituals in attempt to extent life. Now after centuries someone has resurrected the practice again," she said with an ominous tone.

"So they're killing because of…why?" Sam asked still confused.

"Every time they kill a person they harvest their life essence to use for their rituals. The spirit element is the least known and the hardest to capture. That's why we must stop all of them, or they'll recruit another one to join them and never stop killing innocent women," she finished explaining.

"You okay honey?" It took him a second to realize it wasn't Alana but his wife's voice.

"Yea babe just sitting here relaxing, trying to get rid of my back pain," he lied.

"I thought I heard you talking," she queried.

"I just turned off the TV babe," another lie.

"You feel up to coming to bed?"

"In a little bit."

"Don't be up too late," she said as she walked over and kissed him.

He waited for a few minutes, "you there?" he asked.

"Always darling," came a ghostly reply.

"That was close, I can't have her thinking I'm talking to myself, she'll have those damn doctors pumping me full of more drugs," he said agitated.

"Don't worry Sam, she loves you and worries about you," Alana told him.

"I know," he said half-heartily.

"What's wrong my darling?" Alana asked hearing his tone change.

"Nothing, I worry too much about her and the kids."

"Don't be, they will never find out," Alana said trying to comfort him.

"Thanks Alana," Sam smiled.

"I will do everything in my power to protect you, for without you there is no hope."

"Hope huh; I guess where there's a will there's a way. So back to Alexander Demarkov; how do we find him?"

"That's why I was gone today, remember."

"Where is he?" Sam asked feeling the excitement as adrenaline started surging through his veins like fire. Why did he suddenly feel so alive?

Alana could see the change in him and was pleased. "He's across town, he doesn't know about Louis yet," she said smiling.

"Good I don't want him to make a run for it," he said smiling also.

"Careful these kinds of men don't run; they are the embodiment of evil," Alana told Sam her smile fading.

"All the better," Sam grinned.

"What do you mean; 'all the better'?" Alana asked him.

"Nothing," he said dismissively.

"Then why are you smiling like that?" she questioned further.

"They deserve their fate," Sam answered, his mind already racing about the upcoming night's entertainment.

"True, they do deserve their fate, but don't get carried away; remember the best intentions can lead us astray." She said encouraging Sam not to take pleasure in their demise.

"I won't," he muttered, thinking about killing Alexander Demarkov. It scared him about how good it felt. Did that make him as evil as they were? How could it when he was bringing justice to the victims? After all he was saving a lot of people a great deal of future grief by preventing these men from killing anyone else. If he did have one redeeming quality it was the fact that he hated to see the innocent suffer.

"Let's go," he told Alana in a hushed voice.

"You sure you're up for this so soon after Carson?"

"Of course, after all the longer we wait, the more he kills."

"Okay," she agreed.

Sam was already getting dressed as he walked to his bedroom door and looked in and saw his beautiful wife sleeping peacefully and smiled. He was a very lucky man to have such a great woman he thought turning and walking back across the living room to leave.

The more he learned about the dark side and all the murderers living in close proximity to his family. It reinforced his determination to kill all these no-good-for-nothing bastards. He would never allow them a chance to harm another living soul. He felt awe-inspired; he would become the Left Hand of God and none would escape his wrath. They would receive their just punishment for their atrocious sins on earth and he would make sure it would be soon.

He started his truck which thankfully was quiet he didn't want to wake anyone up, besides he hated loud-ass vehicles. As he backed out into the street Alana appeared beside him.

"So where we headed?" Sam asked nonchalantly as if they were going on a picnic.

"South End, just off Parson's Avenue. We can't catch him coming home, he's already there," Alana said a little concerned.

"The element of surprise is still there, he doesn't know we're coming to kill him," Sam said confidently.

"Don't under estimate Demarkov Sam he is a brutal person and much stronger than Carson was," Alana warned.

"It's okay, I brought a little extra help this time," he grinned.

"I still worry about you, after all you're flesh and blood, and I'm not."

"True," he agreed.

"His place is just ahead."

He didn't even remember turning onto Parson's Avenue.

"The red brick duplex on the corner," she directed him.

He decided it was best to circle around and recon the area before stopping.

"Where are you going?" Alana asked as he drove past Demarkov's house.

"Just circling around the block to make sure no one's around."

"Oh."

"Don't worry we'll get them," he smiled at her.

The anticipation was killing him; he was like a hunter stalking its prey. Now the filthy murderous scum had become the hunted. The euphoric highs of adrenaline made his senses hyper aware. He could see even the tiniest movement of the birds in a nearby tree; a dog barking three houses down on the left, the creak of the opening the truck door, the smell of the city on a cool autumn night.

He slowly closed his pickup door and looked at the house across the street for any signs of life. No lights were on, he began to wish he had more time for surveillance; however he was great at improvising.

He checked his watch, already fifteen minutes after midnight, which meant fewer chances of being seen. He had to be as quite as possible so none of the neighbors would hear anything and call the police. He had a pair of latex gloves from his truck's first aid kit which he always carried, and then nearly laughed out loud.

"What?" Alana asked.

"Nothing, I just thought it was funny that I carry a first aid kit to help people and now I'm using the gloves from it to make sure I don't leave any fingerprints behind when hurting someone."

He heard a soft musical laugh from Alana.

"Ironic I know," he smirked.

He also brought a small glass cutter that would be perfect for cutting out a small hole in a window so he could unlatch it.

They made their way across the street to the house. He slowly walked up to the door to see if it had and panes of glass or if he had to go through a nearby window. The door was a solid heavy wood door.

"I can't go in with you," Alana told him.

"Why?" Sam asked just above a whisper.

"See the symbols carved across the top of the door frame, those are meant to keep spirits out. I cannot cross the threshold," Alana spoke in a low menacing tone.

"It's okay, I can handle it," Sam whispered to her and then was surprised by the door opening and no one was standing there on the other side, instantly causing every muscle in him to tense.

"Com' in," they heard a male voice with a thick eastern European accent.

"I see you've brought' your spirit bitch," the voice taunted.

Alana's form came into sharp focus crackling with waves of energy.

"I'll show you," Sam heard her said as she headed for the door only to smash into an invisible barrier preventing her from getting through.

The laughter coming from the room made him furious, "your flimsy spirit barrier won't stop me," Sam said walking through the door.

"Good," he heard the voice say coming from a dark figure sitting in a chair directly in front of him. In an instant the man leapt tackling Sam to the ground and striking him hard across the right side of his face. The man howled in pain reeling backwards off him as if he had been struck by lightning. Sam took the opportunity to get to his feet pouncing like a lion. He was on Demarkov in a heartbeat with a kick to his midsection sending him crashing over a nearby table. Yet in a split second Demarkov lunged again, Sam felt a sharp pain tear into left shoulder as he tried to avoid him.

"Lucky shot bastard," Sam growled pushing

Demarkov backwards. This time when he closed in again Sam was ready with a furious right hook sending him crashing to the floor unconscious.

"Damn that hurt," Sam said rubbing his right hand which was already swelling. He knew he broke at least two fingers; he was going to have to make the lead weight smaller before the next time. He slid the weight into his pocket and threw Demarkov's limp body over his right shoulder. He would have to check on his wounded left shoulder later, now he had to get the hell out of there. Surely someone had heard all the commotion and called the law.

"Where are you?" he called out softly. However she wasn't there and thankfully no one else was either.

After looking up and down the street and seeing or hearing nothing he threw the body into the pickup bed and used zip ties to bind his hands and feet and covered him with a heavy tarp.

"Damn it," he cursed under his breath, how in the hell was he going to explain this to Jacquelyn tomorrow.

He climbed into his truck wondering where Alana had gone to, thinking she may have been hurt by that spirit barrier somehow.

"I'm here," Alana said weakly her ghostly form coming into focus beside him as he was making his way down Parson's Avenue.

"I was starting to worry," Sam told her

relieved, taking a turn a little too fast.

"Easy darling we don't want to attract…," she stopped short, "you're hurt," she said breathlessly.

"It's nothing, I'll be okay, I've had worse," he grimaced; it only hurt when he thought about it. His damn hand hurt worse than his shoulder, which only hurt when he moved it; his right hand however throbbed immensely.

"You're bleeding," Alana protested.

"Nothing we can do about it right now, we'll have to wait until we get to the old mill," he reminded her.

Before long he pulled into the old gravel yard of the abandoned steel mill. He got out and walked around to the back of the pickup truck and let the tailgate down and pulled the tarp off. Without warning the slimly bastard sprang on him like a coiled snake sending them both crashing to the ground. Sam got to his feet first and somehow Demarkov leapt at him with a twisted look of satisfaction he lunged at Sam. He braced for the coming impact planning to counter his move by grabbing him around his neck and slamming him to the ground. Yet as he closed in Demarkov was struck by an eerie blue light causing him to flail backwards falling into a lifeless heap.

"Who's the bitch now," Alana said menacingly towering over him.

"Damn that was awesome," Sam told Alana

standing there in amazement.

"Payback."

"Remind me to not piss you off," he told her walking over to Demarkov's body. "Did you kill him?"

"Not yet."

"Good, that's my job," Sam said stooping over and picking up Demarkov.

"It is," Alana said; her form taking on a more transparent look.

"Let's get him inside; too bad you can't help me carry him," Sam said walking towards the timeworn mill. "How did you do that?" Sam asked grunting a little from the strain of carrying Demarkov.

"I'm not your average spirit darling," she purred.

"You're telling me," he said as he stepped through a side door of the cavernous building.

He dropped the body next to the old cauldron were Demarkov would enjoy the same fate as his cohort Carson.

During the dismantling of the mill they had sat a large cauldron used to pour molten steel into molds on rows of gas burners used to re-heat steel slabs before they were sent into the rolling presses. Thankfully Sam knew how to turn on the gas supply to them and as long as he never used too much no one would ever know. He returned a moment later and lit the burners with a peculiar hissing sound they sent dancing blue flames flickering hot and bright.

Just like Carson he thought taking his wire cutters out of his back pocket, too bad the son-of-a-bitch isn't awake he deserved pain before death.

"No Sam it is not up to us to torture him, just simply deal justice. His punishment will come on the other side," Alana said calmly.

"Sorry," Sam said apolitically as he snipped off both of Demarkov's thumbs and re-bound his arms behind him.

Sam raised him up on the hook and pushed him over the top of the now red hot cauldron. As he began to lower him in Demarkov's eyes opened, yet no screams, not one word did he utter. Sam watched him smile as he lowered him into the deep pot. Flames erupted out of the top, even more than that had when he roasted Carson.

"That's odd," Sam noted.

"He was the Avox of fire."

"Like the element?" Sam asked as he sat down to wait he began feeling weak.

"My darling," Alana said sensing his pain floated over closely to his side.

"I'll be alright, I'm tough," he said sitting there holding his bleeding left shoulder with his injured right hand.

"Shhh," he heard Alana in a humming voice, "shhh".

Fragments raced through his mind; a lifetime of; places, people, and events like a high speed projector. An image of a beautiful woman in her mid-twenties with brown hair, brown eyes, who was so familiar to Sam, it was the only image he could hold onto.

"How long have I been out," Sam asked Alana as he came to, trying to get the world back in focus.

"Not long my darling," Alana purred hovering in front on him.

When he moved he was surprised at the lack of pain, maybe his injuries weren't as severe as he thought. He got to his feet regaining his composure and looked down at his right hand which looked and felt normal when he flexed it. He took it up to his wounded left shoulder; there was a hole through his jacket and shirt which both were blood stained yet only a tender pink patch of skin was where the stab wound was. At least he wasn't losing his mind.

"How?" He asked his fingers tracing the outline of the former wound.

"I mended your injuries while you were out. I couldn't have my darling hurt," she purred lovingly.

"Thank you; I had no idea how I was going to explain that tomorrow. What time is it?"

"Two thirty."

"Damn we got to get a move on," Sam said urgently heading over to shut the gas off. It was a bitch getting Demarkov's ashes out the still hot cauldron. He used a small metal bucket mounted to a long iron pole nearly getting burned in the process.

"Careful darling," Alana warned.

"Got it," he said climbing down off the platform next to the top of the crucible.

It was amazing to see how extreme heat had transformed Demarkov's body into fine powdery ashes with no bone fragments. Sam knew exactly what to do next.

Chapter 9 Consequences

James had a terrible time sleeping waking up every hour on the hour until finally getting up at five. Guess it was the upcoming meeting with Captain Harris, besides the fact that he was still trying to figure out all these new feelings he was having toward Sarah. Hell he had just met her and was acting like a damn teenager with raging hormones. Before long he shaved; showered, and was out the door.

He was still feeling nervousness in the pit of his stomach as he walked into the precinct.

"Get your ass in here," he heard the Captain's voice from across the empty office.

"Yes Captain," Colburn answered heading towards Harris' office.

He entered into the Captain's office and stood in front of his desk. There was no use to sit down this wasn't going to be a social call.

"Well?" Captain Harris asked impatiently, causing him to stand straighter. He always tried to think before he spoke.

"Well Colburn you going to stand there all damn morning?" Captain Harris demanded, a vein started to bulge in his right temple.

"Sorry Captain," Colburn stammered.

He gave him a full report of yesterday's events, leaving out Breckenridge's meeting with the mayor.

"Is that all, shit for brains?" Harris said now turning red. He knew something was getting ready to hit the fan.

"Sir, if it's about the leak to the press, I have no idea who it could be," Colburn said thinking that must be it.

"Detective Colburn do you take me for a fool?"
"Sir."

"Who the fuck do you think you're dealing with," now Harris had veins popping out of his neck too.

"Excuse me sir."

"Sir HELL!" Harris shouted.

"Colburn I know Detective Breckenridge had a meeting with the mayor yesterday evening. Why did you leave that part out of your report? That's why I assigned you to work with her," Harris told him with a look of dissatisfaction.

"I'm…," Colburn started to protest.

"Breckenridge is the FUCKING mayor's daughter Colburn in case you didn't know. I didn't get to where I am today by having my head up my ass, LIKE YOU!" he screamed the last part.

He had stopped listening after the part about Sarah being the mayor's daughter. Why in the hell didn't she tell him?

"The only reason I don't bust your ass right back down to traffic beat, is because of the personal request from the mayor that you work the case with Detective Breckenridge. From now on when I ask you for a report you make damn sure you tell me everything. Do I make myself clear?" Harris demanded.

"Yes sir, anything else?" Colburn said stiffly.

"Yes I want you at the press conference this morning with me and the Chief of Police."

"Sir?"

"You heard me; he has requested both you and Breckenridge to be there this morning, defer any questions to her."

"Yes sir."

"Knock it off with that Sir bullshit; I work for a living. Whether you realize it or not Colburn I was busting crooks before you were born and regardless of what you think of me; you can trust me," his temper gone. "I need someone to depend on. I know your record and I think I can trust you; can I?" Captain asked.

"Yes of course Captain, I'm sorry I didn't tell you everything; I will not do it again."

"See that you don't; and for the love of god, make damn sure nothing happens to Breckenridge."

"Yes sir, err sorry Captain," Colburn backtracked on calling him sir.

He walked out of the Captain's office with a mixture of confusion and anger. He had underestimated Harris for sure and felt like a complete fool. It wouldn't happen again he promised himself grinding his teeth opening the case file on his desk. He couldn't concentrate on it though; why hadn't she told him? Would he have? It still didn't make a difference about how he felt about her. None of that mattered right now; he had to get a handle on this strange case.

"Good morning," Sarah said brightly, causing him to look up, "glad to see you're reading up on the case."

"Yep," he didn't mean to sound so angry.

"What's wrong?" she could tell something was up.

"Captain rip your ass that bad?" she asked.

"No," he lied.

"Then what?" she asked again.

"Just learned some interesting facts about you, that's all."

She knew immediately, "James I didn't tell you because; first I just met you and didn't know if I could trust you to keep your mouth shut. And second I don't want anyone to know and I don't want to be treated differently. Do you know how hard it is being the mayor's daughter and a detective on top of that?"

"I wouldn't have treated you any different," James said his anger deflating.

"Bullshit," she smiled.

God he couldn't be mad at her, she was too damn beautiful.

"Look James we got a lot of ground to cover before the press conference. However will you do me one favor?" Sarah asked sincerely.

"What?"
"Please don't breathe a word about my relationship to thc major with anyone. I've worked hard to get where I am and done it on my own without help from my father and I don't want it all wrecked now."

"My lips are sealed," James swore.

"Good," Sarah said smiling.

"Damn," she said glancing up at the clock on

the wall.

"What?"

"Almost time for the press conference," Sarah said getting up.

"Shit," James said getting up from his desk. "Hell I don't have anything to be worried about it's your case and if anything goes wrong I'll just blame you," James said jokingly.

"You're the rookie," she laughed, "and they get blamed for everything."

"Very funny," James retorted; following her out to the press conference feeling like he was walking to the gallows.

This would be the first press conference he ever attended and even though he didn't have to worry about answering any questions he still felt nervous. He stood to the left of the small podium that had been set up. He was trying not to lock his knees and pass out, god that would be so embarrassing; he would never live it down.

Most of the questions were being directed at the Chief of Police with a few being deferred to Sarah for answers; who seemed right at home answering without hesitation. He was so lost in thought it took him a minute to realize she had stopped speaking and was looking at the reporters who were snapping pictures over to the left side of the steps.

Suddenly they heard someone from the throng

of reporters that it had happened again. Sarah,
with Harris and the Chief in tow walked down the
stairs to find out what all the commotion was about.
There next to the concrete foundation were a pile of
ashes with an envelope and what looked to be a
human thumb lying on top of it. All hell broke loose
with every one of the news reporters vying to get the
best shot.

"Everyone back up!" Captain Harris yelled.
"Colburn get some uniforms out here and get this
area sealed off now."

"Yes Captain," James said and took off
running into the precinct.

Back outside they finally got the news crews
pushed back and the scene taped off.

"Colburn, Breckenridge; my office now,"
Captain Harris ordered.

"Yes Captain," both said heading back into the
precinct behind him.

Harris slammed his office door closed so hard
that the window exploded.

"I don't care what you do; find this sick son-
of-a-bitch, use every resource we have. Got it!"
Harris screamed and headed into the main office
area. By now all the detectives were standing at their
desk.

"Now that I have your fucking attention; I
want to know how in the hell a room full of
detectives walked right by that pile of ashes this

morning on your way in. ARE YOU ALL YOU FUCKING BLIND!" Harris was nearly turning purple in the face now. "I want a damn security camera installed out there TODAY! Oh and by the way, thanks a whole fucking lot to whoever leaked the first one to the damn press. Now we all look like a bunch of fucking morons and can someone get maintenance down here," Captain Harris fumed and headed back to his office stepping through the broken out center instead of opening it and then yelled, "Colburn, Breckenridge get your asses out there and get me some answers."

"Holy hell, he's pissed," James told Sarah as they walked back outside.

"I thought he was going to have a coronary," Sarah joked.

"No such luck," James said ducking under the police tape behind her. They put on their latex gloves, CSU was already there, there was no use in calling the medical examiner, they were no way in hell he would be able to determine a cause of death or do an autopsy.

"Might as well save him the drive and send the remains up to the lab and get them analyzed to see if they're human," James said.

"Hmm this doesn't look like normal cremated remains," she told him.

"What do you mean?"

"These ashes are very fine with no noticeable

bone fragments, normally when a person is cremated their remains some pieces of bone and after they take them out of the oven they have to use a grinder to grind down the big chucks."

That made James cringe, "you sure know a lot about this stuff, he told her."

"I read a lot," Sarah said taking out an evidence bag and placed the severed thumb in it.

"Looks like a human thumb most likely male," showing it to him.

"Umm hmm," he agreed.

Then she gently picked up the envelope which wasn't sealed, so she open it a pulled out a letter that was inside.

It was a plain type written letter that read:

Your welcome,

I give you the remnants of one Alexander Demarkov – A Murderer. The remains of his victims can be found buried in the southeast part of the abandoned lot of the South End Drive In.

VK

"Just like the first one," Sarah said reaching it to Catherine the head CSU team.

"Here run the letter and envelope for prints also run the thumb's DNA and print to see if it's in our system. Have the ashes analyzed to see if they're human, ASAP. We are going to find out who is doing this and put an end to it before we have every vigilante lunatic in the damn city out doing this," Breckenridge said firmly.

"Now that its hit the papers, god help us," James agreed.

Chapter 10 Sam and Alana

"You going to be okay with the house all to yourself today?" Jacquelyn teased.

"I don't know," Sam said grabbing her around her waist hugging her tightly.

"Hello beautiful; I love you," he whispered as he kissed her.

"Love you too; it's good to see you in a good mood and taking my advice," she smiled.

"Feels good to take some time off," he lied concealing the real reason.

"I'll call you at lunch," she told him grabbing her work bag.

They hugged and kissed again as he opened the front door seeing her off.

"Chivalry's not dead," Alana purred as Sam watched Jacquelyn back out of the driveway.

"Of course not," he replied closing the door.

"I would open the door for you, except you don't need it," he said smiling.

"True," Alana laughed in that musical tone he loved.

"Now we're alone I have some questions about last night."

"Okay," Alana said brightly.

"Why did Demarkov fly backwards off me when he punched me? Did you do something?"

"Remember when I kissed you on your cheek?"

"Yes, but I thought that was just to show me that you were real."

"It was, but I also placed a protective mark upon you, however the effect has never been that strong before."

"What do you mean before?"

"Sam darling you're not my first, she purred seductively, "I've helped others before you."

"How did you heal me?" Sam asked, his hand going to his left shoulder absentmindedly.

"I am growing stronger darling with each kill," she teased. "Darling why are you so lost in thought?"

she asked.

"An image of a woman from my past, last night when I was out a lot of things went through my mind, but her face is stuck," Sam said half mumbling.

Alana knew he was remembering his long lost sister.

"She is the reason I was called forth to aid you, and why you are the path you're on," Alana said her tone changing ever so slightly to a more serious one.

"Who is she?" Sam asked getting agitated.

"It is not for me to tell you. You must remember on your own," Alana told him tenderly.

"WHY?" He demanded losing his temper.

"Sam, my darling, because only then will it be real to you," Alana answered softly, causing his temper to ease.

"I'm sorry."

"I understand, but please be patient. I promise you darling you will have the answers you seek."

"I'll try my best," Sam promised.

"We must see my Nabila today."

"Where is she?"

"Not far from here."

"Well what are we waiting for, let's go," Sam said as he got up to get his keys.

It wasn't long before they were pulling into the driveway of a familiar place.

"I've been here before."

"Yes you have," Alana smiled.

"So this is where your Nabila is? It says Spirit Advisor on the sign, isn't that like palm readers?"

"No, they are much more than simple gypsies."

"I always thought they were frauds."

"Some are," Alana said as Sam got out of the truck and walked up to the front door which opened before he could knock.

"Sam! I'm so glad you're here. Come in dear, come in," the old woman said breathlessly ushering him inside the little house.

He knew her and this place; he just couldn't put his finger on how or why.

"I've been here before," Sam muttered.

"Yes dear you have, many times. My name is Marlena. Please sit and make yourself comfortable." She said pointing to an old couch with floral patterns with an afghan throw over the back. "Can I get you anything to drink?"

"No thanks," he was dying to get to the bottom

of it.

"Very well," she answered him and then sat down in a nearby arm chair.

"I see you've begun remembering with Alana's help," Marlena said. He was caught off guard to be asked about someone who no one else could see.

"I am the one who brought her into this realm to help you."

"So you're a Nabila?"

"Yes, but I like to go by Marlena," she said with a little laugh.

"Why do you seem so familiar to me? Do we know each other?" Sam asked.

"Is he ready?" Marlena asked Alana who was standing next to him.

"He is," Alana answered in a somber tone.

With a nod she began. "The reason I am familiar to you is that you and my son were best friends." Marlena said.

"What do you mean?"

"He passed away several years ago," Marlena told him leaving out the fact her son died in the accident that nearly killed Sam.

"I'm sorry for your loss, I wish I could remember him," Sam said honestly.

"After you were out of rehabilitation you would stop by often, confused and stressed trying to find answers to your past," Marlena continued.

Sam was growing frustrated. "This isn't helping Alana. Why are we here?"

"Be patient darling, the answers are forth coming," Alana assured him.

"Sam the reason I summoned Alana to help you was not to remember my son, it was so you can avenge," she hesitated, "to avenge your sister's death," Marlena's voice now trembling.

"WHAT KIND OF BULLSHIT IS THIS?" Sam shouted rising to his feet. "I would know if I had a sister after all I remember my brother Roger!" He could feel himself getting light-headed.

"Sam, please!" Marlena pleaded.

"Please hell…" Sam started to say when Alana cut him off.

"Sit down," she told him firmly, "she has the answers you seek."

"Why? Why in the hell didn't my family tell me?" Sam said shaking his head and sitting back down on the old couch.

"They didn't think you could handle it. You barely survived the accident and they were afraid it would kill you," Marlena explained.

"But how could I have completely forgotten

her?" Sam said his mind numbed by the horrific news.

"Darling it is her face you remembered last night. You are strong enough now," Alana added.

"Where is she? Why haven't I seen her?" Sam questioned, his mind racing.

"She died," Marlena's words struck him like a thunderbolt. His mind whirled uncontrollably.

"What?" He felt sick.

Marlena hurried and got a cold washcloth. "Easy dear, easy."

"EASY HELL!" He was furious, his head throbbing, heart beating so rapidly it felt like exploding. "Why hasn't my FUCKING so called family told me this?" He screamed in blind rage. He should have known; no one had the right to withhold that information from him. He had to get a hold of himself it wasn't Marlena's fault.

"So I've been coming here because your son was my best friend and I was trying to contact my dead sister?" Sam asked stunned by the revelations.

"You came to me searching for answers," Marlena answered.

"Then why can't I remember?"
"You were too weak dear. And every time I thought you were strong enough I would tell you and you would get so upset you'd have another spell and I'd have to call your father. Sam your family was just

trying to protect you, after all you've been through so much," Marlena said through tear stained eyes.

"Please don't," Sam spoke softly seeing how upset she was. "I'm sorry about my temper," he forced himself to calm down.

"That's the reason I summoned Alana to aid you, I knew you could never do it alone," Marlena sobbed.

"You're right, please don't cry," Sam said tenderly reaching her a handkerchief.

"Thank you, you've always been such a gentleman," Marlena said accepting the soft white linen handkerchief.

He had let himself grow too weak, inwardly criticizing the way he had behaved. *Get a fucking grip man*, he'd been through hell and back and there wasn't a damn thing he couldn't handle.

"So…" he steadied himself, "you were telling me about my sister. Is that why I've been coming here all these years?" he asked.

"Yes," Marlena answered wiping her eyes.

"Why? Was it to try to communicate with her?"

"Each time you would stop, was when you had a memory about my son or your sister you would stop and ask me questions about them. Most of the time it didn't go well and you'd have a spell."

"How often would I come?"

"Two or three times a year since the accident."

"And I wouldn't remember the prior times I'd been here?"

"No dear, I hoped one day you would and now I believe you will," Marlena said finally composing herself.

"What happened to my sister, how did she die?"

"No one knows for sure, she disappeared the day of your accident. Her car was found in the parking lot outside of her work place. Your parents filed a missing person's report, but nothing was ever found out about her case. After a couple of years they assumed the worst."

"But no one knows for sure?" Sam cut in.

"No, but…" Marlena started when Sam cut her off.

"But what, there's still hope!"

"Darling," this time it was Alana speaking, "she's on my side."

He sat there for a long moment unsure of what to say or how to act learning the fact that his sister went missing the same day he nearly died in the accident and on top of that he had a best friend who is also dead. And he couldn't remember a FUCKING thing, except for the face of his long lost sister. He felt more anger and rage than grief; at least if they weren't dead he would be able to get to know them again. And then there's his family, what the hell were they doing to him? If they had told him sooner maybe he would have remembered them; maybe that would have jarred his damaged brain into fucking working again. Damn it, damn it, he fought for control feeling the raging beast of pure unadulterated rage welling up inside like an awakening volcano. He drew in another deep breath, "what was her name?"

"Elizabeth," Alana answered.

Now he a name to put with the face; one that would haunt him the rest of his life. One thing was for certain, he was going to find out what happened to her, even if it killed him.

"Sam darling please know that we are on the road to discovering the answers you seek," Alana said firmly.

"We will," Sam spoke gritting his teeth, making an inward vow.

"Is that why we have been going after those men, Alana?" Sam asked.

"Yes."

"Which one had something to do with my sister's death?" Sam asked doing his best to remain composed.

"Logar Grunin, he's the most powerful and the leader of the five, he is chief over the fifth element of spirit."

"Why didn't we kill him first?" Sam asked impatiently.

"You weren't ready and I was not strong enough yet. Don't worry darling he will die soon once we kill his last two associates, which will weaken him and make him easier to take out."

"I don't want fucking easy I want my sister's killer to pay!" Sam screamed, his head now splitting with pain. Marlena ran to get another cold washcloth thinking he was going to pass out again.

"I'm fine, I'll be even better when Logar Grunin is dead."

"You will my darling, you will," Alana purred her words having a calming effect on him.

"Who are the two we have to kill before Logar?"

"Markius Kingston and Victor Vorgol."

"You said each man is linked to an element; how?" Sam asked Alana.

"Each one kills their victim according to the element they worship. Carlson's was earth, he buried his victims alive; Demarkov's was fire, he would burn his to death. That leaves Markius who is water he drowns his, and Victor's is air, he suffocates his. Finally Logar's is spirit. I'm unsure how he kills his victims because he weaves shadows surrounding his vile work. One reason we must kill his companions first so that he will reveal himself."

"I see," Sam said turning to Marlena. "Can you summon or talk to my sister?"

"I've tried many times, but her spirit is hidden from me in the shadow, that's why I summoned Alana to help you. Things are visible to her that is not to me," Marlena added.

"We will avenge her and deal justice my darling," Alana reassured him.

"Marlena thank you for everything you've done, but I must go now," Sam said getting to his feet.

"Please can you stay a little while longer?"

"I'm sorry, but I've got a lot of work to do. Although I can't remember your son, I'm sure he was a good man; he has a great mother," Sam smiled.

"Ah my sweet Sam; my sweet Sam thank you," Marlena said through teary eyes grabbing him in a tight hug, he hugged her back.

"David," Sam said slowly as if to himself.

"What did you say?" Marlena asked shaken.

"David, does that name mean anything to you?"

"That was my son's name," Marlena said stepping back drying her eyes. "I knew one day you would remember him, I knew you would."

"Don't get your hopes up just yet, I only remembered a name," Sam told her gently.

"It's a start my sweet Sam," she said smiling.

Sam made his way to the front door promising Marlena he'd return as soon as he could.

He never spoke on the drive home and Alana didn't bother him knowing he needed time to digest everything he had learned today.

The phone was ringing as he walked through the door. Sam grabbed the phone, the caller ID was Jacquelyn's cell. The last person he wanted to talk to right now. However he acted as if nothing had happened, thankfully the conversation was brief.

"Darling your family loves you and was only doing what they thought was best for you. Don't be hard on them," Alana said after he hung up the phone.

"I'll deal with that later, right now we have more important things to do," Sam said in a hollow tone.

Chapter 11 Cops

"That was the CSU's office; they have the DNA results in. It's a match to the sample we got from Miranda's mother," Colburn told Breckenridge as soon as he hung up.

"So our killer knew Carlson and Miranda, or knew what Carlson had done."

"So what's the motive? Why not just turn Carlson in? Why go through all this? Do they have a vendetta against him?"

"The one thing that frightens me is how our suspect found out about Carlson and now Demarkov. I had my suspicions Carlson was working with others, perhaps a cult or sick religious nuts. I should have pieced this together sooner," she said flatly.

"You're doing a hell-of-a job, don't beat yourself up," Colburn said encouragingly.

"Thanks James," she said genuinely.

After giving final instructions to the CSU team they left for the M.E.'s office.

"We cannot afford to have any more fuckups."

"Agreed," James said hating the thought of facing Captain Harris again.

"James I know I probably don't need to tell you this," Sarah began when James cut her off.

"Oh god!" James burst out. "You don't love me; I knew it."

"My, don't we have a sense of humor?"

"Just trying to lighten the mood."

She smiled, "I appreciate the effort, however getting back to what I was saying. Please be extremely careful who you talk to and I will do the same. We damn sure don't need anything getting to the press."

"Don't worry Sarah I'll only rat you out to Captain Harris," James said laughing. "After all he's my hero."

"He's not one to play games with."

"Trust me I've already learned that the hard way."

"Good," she said as she pulled into the parking

garage of the M.E.'s office.

"Why are we going to the medical examiner's office? There's no way to determine the cause of death, much less anything else for that matter."

"The more we know about what little we have will help us, besides you never know what may turn up," she answered as they walked into the exam room. A middle aged, slightly overweight balding white man in green scrubs was working on the body of Miranda Emerson.

"Hello detectives, I'm Dr. Ray Daniels."

It was Sarah who spoke first, "I'm Detective Breckenridge and this is my partner Detective Colburn."

"Nice to meet you both, I was just finishing up a pathology report on our victim. I saw the news this morning. Is it true?" Daniels asked.

"Afraid so," Sarah answered and then without getting into detail she went on. "Was you able to determine the cause of death?"

"There were no noticeable wounds from anything man-made. No drugs were detected in her hair. She suffered from some type of crushing injury to her upper chest which caused several broken ribs one of which punctured her lungs leading to her death."

"Was she struck by a blunt object?"

"No, there's no isolated point of impact or

bruising of tissue that indicate any blunt force trauma. It's as if her entire chest had been compress by something."

"Would be buried alive cause that?"

"It would, I've seen injuries like this from construction workers who died during cave-ins from the weight of the earth. It's possible someone done this to our victim"

"What have you found out about the ashes that were brought in?" Sarah asked as if grilling a suspect for every tidbit of information she could possible get.

"Not much, the chemical composition does match what you would find in cremated human remains, yet it could also come from a biological animal with enough mass to simulate the amount we have. If we have all of the remains and they are in fact human. The remains would approximate an average human of one hundred and eighty to two hundred pounds. They are no bone fragments or other foreign material in the ashes. It would take an extreme amount of heat to reduce a human body to the consistency of these ashes. The thumb is a left thumb of a human male." Daniels finished.

"The print we took from it at the precinct confirmed in belonged to Alexander Demarkov, who had a prior conviction for assault two years ago. We're trying to find his last known residence now," Breckenridge told Daniels.

"However based on what I have, I cannot rule Demarkov is deceased," Daniels added.

"What the hell are you talking about?" Colburn asked.

"Detective, other than a thumb and a pile of ashes, I have no body, no way of knowing anything. You have no crime scene where he was killed, no witnesses, and no murder weapon. Hell for all we know Demarkov is still alive, just missing a thumb same as Carlson's," Daniels said firmly.

"Great let's put out an APB on a middle-aged white guy who's missing his left thumb," James said feeling like they were getting nowhere.

"Whoever done this did not use a standard crematory oven, they simply can't get hot enough. Look into places that use high temperature kilns or furnaces like steel mills," Daniels added trying to help.

"After you get done have the ashes and thumb sent over to our CSU team. Call me as soon as you have the report ready," Breckenridge told him.

"Yes ma'am," Daniels replied curtly.

"I'll notify Mrs. Emerson of the DNA results. When will she be able to claim her daughter's body?"

"I'm finishing up the report today and will be able to release the body tomorrow," Daniels answered.

"Thanks, please call me if anything new turns up."

"No problem, you'll be the first to know," Daniels replied in a sharp crisp voice betraying his age.

"Let's go to the Emerson's place I prefer to tell her in person and I have a few more questions for her," Sarah told James as she headed out the door of the exam room.

"Okay," he agreed, even though he didn't relish the thought of it. At least Sarah would be doing the talking.

James was about to ask her a question when her cell phone rang.

"Detective Breckenridge," she answered.

"Have the CSU ready but do not enter the premises until I get there," she said before sliding the phone back into her coat pocket.

"They found the last known address of Demarkov."

"We are heading there now and then we'll go to the Emerson's home."

"Sounds good, hopefully we can catch a break on this crazy case," James said earnestly.

"How are we going to prove that Carlson and Demarkov are dead?" James asked as he got into the driver's seat of his unmarked cruiser.

"As far as Carlson goes, hopefully we can find more evidence that he was murdered, same with

Demarkov. We have to find out for sure otherwise we're never going to solve this case," Sarah told him getting lost in thought as he drove.

"Left up here on twenty second street," she said looking at the GPS on her smartphone.

"Now hang a right on Elm Street in two blocks, house number is three hundred and thirty-one," she told him putting her phone away.

"Not much to look at," James noted as they got out of the unmarked cruiser.

"Careful, looks can be deceiving, never take anything for granted when you're a detective," Sarah said with a somber tone.

"Sounds like you don't have a very good feeling about what we are going to find inside?" James queried.

"Do you?"

"Nope."

"I'll take the front," Colburn said pulling his service weapon out.

"I'll head around to see if they are a back door," she nodded and headed around the side of the house.

He gave her time before yelling; "POLICE! OPEN THE DOOR!"

Colburn waited a few seconds and yelled again, no answer. He tried the door knob, it was unlocked. He slowly opened the door enough to peek inside and go in with a tight grip on his pistol ready to fire in a heartbeat.

There were signs of a struggle; the front room was torn apart. He saw Breckenridge coming in from the back he holstered his weapon.

"Looks like there was quite a fight here," she said as she put her weapon away.

"We may be able to get some prints or other forensic evidence that will help us to solve these vendetta killings," she said as she put on latex gloves; James followed suit so he wouldn't contaminate the crime scene.

"So you think we have a vendetta killer on our hands?" he asked.

"That's the way the evidence is pointing right now; at least now you've gave our killer a name."

"Huh?"

"From now on we will call our suspect The Vendetta Killer, better than John Doe and it fits the initials VK on the letters."

"Your case, your call, let's just make sure that we catch the one responsible for making us look like idiots."

"Let's get to it, shall we?" Sarah said as her attention was drawn to the white spots on the carpet to their left.

"What causes these kinds of spots?" James ask looking it over.

"Probable bleach, they must have been blood there and our killer is trying to cover his tracks," she said as she got down on one knee to take a closer look.

"See this spot here; it has a pinkish hue in the middle. Make sure CSU takes the entire rug, I want it gone over with fine tooth comb in case there are any traces of our victim or suspect."

"Wonder if Demarkov has a secret chamber of horror like Carlson did?" James asked with a grimace.

"Let's find out," Sarah answered getting to her feet. "I'll take the down stairs, you take the upstairs."

"Sounds good to me," James said happily, after all he was less likely to find sadistic shit upstairs he thought.

As he walked up the stairs every one of the old steps creaked, causing him to pull out weapon and approach more tensely than he would normally do. Why did all these psychopaths have normal looking houses on the outside at least? There was nothing upstairs except two bedrooms and a small bathroom; nothing to tie Demarkov or anyone else to a crime. The rooms looked barley used and was sparsely furnished. So he headed back down to check on what Sarah may have found.

"Where are you?" James asked out loud not

seeing her anywhere downstairs.

"Down here," he heard her call out. Her voice was coming through an opened door leading into the basement. Great he thought to himself here we go again, heading down the stairs, hoping this wasn't a sign of things to come. Yet this is what he wanted to do more than anything, bring justice to families, he was going to have to toughen up and get used to the grisly business of investigating the worst of the worst. He knew deep down he could do it, he just had to keep a level head and not let it get personal.

"Coming," he called down the stairwell.

The short steep stairwell led down to a completely dark basement. He pulled out his flashlight and switched it on and saw Sarah was in the far corner with her light shining on a spot on the floor.

"Find something?" He asked walking over to her.

"Maybe, I'm trying to figure out how to work this switch."

"Been easier if you had turned on the lights."

"There was no light switch that I could find anywhere, genius" she replied smartly. "Here, push down and twist this knob to the right," she told him while she held the flashlight.

As soon as he did they heard a click a few feet away and a bright light came on from overhead temporary blinding them, taking a few seconds for their eyes to get adjusted.

"Holy shit; what in the hell was this guy into?" James exclaimed.

"Apparently the one who worships fire," Sarah spoke in amazement looking around the room. "Wow, every wall is covered with ancient symbols all surrounding the fire symbol in the middle. I've never seen anything like this before," she said in astonishment.

"I've only seen shit like this in the movies," James said still trying to make sense of everything.

"Look at the gilded sun image above the altar. It was worshipped since the dawn of man and considered by alchemists to be the first manifestation of fire. It's clear this was Demarkov's element."

"What's that heavy metal cabinet in the corner? It looks like some kind of upright oven." James asked as he walked over and stood in front of it.

"It is, it's how he killed his victims," Sarah replied looking closer at it.

"By burning them to death and disposing of their remains after he killed them?"

"Don't you understand, each of these men was killing according to the alchemy element they worshiped? Now it's making sense; they were trying to gather something, like an essence, by the way they killed their victims'."

"You mean like witches would?"

"Kind of, in the earliest form of voodoo the way you killed something would determine the type of essence you got during the ritual."

"I think we need a priest or something," James said still in disbelief of what he was seeing.

"Don't be silly, this stuff only has power over those who put faith in it."

"Do you?"

"I believe people are capable of committing terrible acts of evil, and also by the same token people can do great good."

"But why are our suspects doing this?"

"In a delusional attempt to fulfill their desires and overcome fear of their own death."

"Just my luck, my first homicide case is a cult of devil worshipers."

"Not devil James; I've never seen anything like this, they are blending alchemy and Voodoo, but I can tell you that it has nothing to do with the worship of Satan."

"You're the expert."

"This is out of my league; we're going to have to call the FBI in on it. They have the resources we need to be able to close this case before things get a lot worse."

"Looks like there are bones mixed in with the ashes, from the looks of it there are remains in here from multiple victims."

"If Demarkov wasn't already dead this would fit his M.O."

"Yeah but think, if our killer knew how Demarkov killed his victims, and so now he's using the same method to take them out to get revenge."

"Do you think it could be an ex-cult member doing this?" James asked.

"That makes sense; a former member would have intimate knowledge of the inner workings of the group."

"Either way I don't think the killings are going to stop unless we catch those behind the cult and their killer," James added.

"For our sake I hope we get to them before anymore killings happen," Sarah said sounding weary.

"You don't sound very positive," James observed.

"Sorry feeling a little overwhelmed, this case was difficult enough when I was dealing with what I thought was one serial killer and now we're dealing with an insane alchemy-voodoo cult and someone with one hell-of-a vendetta to settle to top it off."

"It may make our job harder, but not impossible," James told her doing his best to reassure her.

"True, I thought Carlson's place was over the top, but look at the way this room is constructed, it's like a temple," she starred in awe.

"We could spend a week in here."

"We need to get CSU back out Carlson's house."

"Why?" James asked surprised.

"Since we are now dealing with more than we thought, I want to make sure we didn't miss anything also Demarkov's cult members may try to go back and collect artifacts. I want both houses under surveillance."

"At this rate we are going to run out of CSU units."

"We'll have to do the best we can. The Chief of Police has been notified and has called in help from the Ohio State Police for additional manpower. Our case is now top priority," Sarah finished.

"Good maybe we can solve it before anyone else dies," James said.

"CSU will be here in a few minutes, let's go we have a lot of ground to cover," Sarah said briskly.

"You bet."

As soon as they were in the car she was on her phone again. James only heard her responses.

"Thanks for seeing us on short notice," she said before hanging up.

"Where we going?"

"To see Dr. Vorgol the professor of religious studies at OSU, he's one of the smartest people I know in ancient religions. I was in several of his classes when I was in college. We have a meeting at 5:30 p.m. today. That will give us time to go and see Mrs. Emerson and give her the news of her daughter," she added while he was driving.

"This Dr. Vorgol, how is he going to be able to help us in this case?"

"Some of the writing I saw was Cuneiform, it was written by Sumerians thousands of years ago. It's a dead language and only studied, I've never seen it used like the way it is with alchemy."

"I thought alchemy was formed during the Dark Ages in Europe far away and long after the Sumerians, and even then people just trying to turn lead into gold?"

"I'm impressed James I had no ideal you knew so much about history? You're right about the gap in distance and time that passed, however many of the earliest alchemist sought after the Elixir of Life. Only the Philosophers Stone could make the elixir as well as transmute lead into gold. Therefore they could have unimaginable wealth and immorality. It's thought by some that was the reason that Ponce de Leon's mythical search for the Fountain of Youth was fueled by his belief in alchemy."

James really enjoyed listening to talk so passionately like a teacher yearning to pass on knowledge, who just happened to wear a badge.

"You listening James?" She asked looking over at him thinking he wasn't listening.

"Yep; alchemy, Sumerians, fountain of youth; I'm with you."

"Good."

"If you know so much; why do we have to see this professor?"

"He knows more than I do, also he may be able to point us in the right direction to catch our killer. He runs in the circle and has students who may know what's going on in the city, especially cult activity."

"And in turn tell him?" James said with a little sarcasm.

"They don't have too, he is very observant and will know if any of his students are into anything."

"Look at the time we got to be going," James told Sarah looking at his watch.

"You're right let's head there now and then we can compare notes later," Sarah told him as she turned down High Street.

Chapter 12 Sam

"So we need to go after Kingston next?" Sam asked, more of a statement than a question, reassuring himself of his next step.

"Yes darling he should be the next," Alana purred with a hint of musical excitement.

"You sound like you're enjoying this?" Sam asked noticing her tone.

"Darling I always enjoy seeing justice dealt to those who deserve it," Alana said lightly.

"Me too," he smiled in spite of himself. He didn't enjoy the act of killing; or did he? Was it really justice he was after?

"You're not evil," Alana purred as if reading his mind.

"How do you know?"

"If you were I would have not been sent to aid you," Alana simply stated.

"Ever since the accident; I…" he struggled.

"What my darling Sam?" Alana asked softly.

"It's just, I don't feel or think like normal people; right and wrong I mean," he said getting confused.

"Your heart is pure," Alana told him firmly.

"But are my intentions?"

"Darling you are not troubled by the trivial matters of morality. You see the greater good and are willing to do what is necessary to achieve it."

"Perhaps," he answered lost in thought.

"What's wrong?" Alana asked seeing his distraction.

"Nothing."

"Sam darling I may be a spirit, but I can see you're troubled."

"How could I have forgotten her?" Sam asked in a heavy voice filled with sorrow and regret.

"Don't despair my love, you are strong enough now to remember and soon we will avenge her death and free her spirit. You will see justice," Alana comforted him.

"Yes we will!" Sam said slamming his fist down on the coffee table nearly breaking it in half.

"When?"

"Soon," Alana purred.

"Good the faster we get to Kingston and Vorgol the sooner I get to Logar. He will pay dearly for the murder of my sister," Sam spoke through gritted teeth.

"Yes he will, but please don't let the lust of vengeance take over your soul," she warned.

"As long as I get him, I don't give a damn."

"Darling, never stop caring."

He glanced at the clock on the wall, "damn," he said noticing what time it was.

"What?"

"Jacquelyn will be home soon. I want this guy so bad, I hate wasting time. Do you know where to find Kingston?" Sam asked.

Alana hesitated.

"Well?" Sam asked again.

"Yes… but don't you want to wait a little while?"

"It would be best to act before the cops figure out the connections between the five," Sam said bluntly.

"And not your thirst for vengeance?" Alana asked coyly.

"Of course not," he said, his smile betraying his statement.

"Okay we'll go out tonight," Alana relented.

"We have a date then," Sam responded enthusiastically.

"What are you going to do about Jacquelyn? You can't keep sneaking out at night; she's going to catch you and then what?"

"You got a point, but it's too late for me to come up with an excuse to get away tonight. We will have to sneak out and be extra careful. Where's Kingston live? Is it far from here?"

"Not far, down off the waterfront in downtown off Main Street, I can show you."

A flash of pure anger washed over Sam's face.

"What's wrong darling?"

"Thinking about her," he grunted, he didn't have to say her name. Alana knew he was thinking of his sister.

"Darling I make this vow to you; her blood shall be avenged. The blood of the wicked will be shed to atone for the murders they have committed," Alana swore in a deadly tone.

"I will repay," he started to say before Alana cut in.

"We will repay," she corrected, causing him to smile.

"Yes we will," Sam smiled with a wild look in his eyes.

It wasn't long before Jacquelyn was home with the kids in tow behind her.

"Hi babe," Sam said smiling.

"Hi hun," Jacquelyn said before getting interrupted; "hi daddy," they said in unison running at him, each one hugging a leg as he squatted down to hug them.

"Did you guys have a good day?" He asked, silently thinking to himself how fast they were growing up, seemed like yesterday they were wearing diapers.

"It was fun daddy; Grammy let us help make cookies. Here I saved you one," Cassie said reaching into her school backpack.

"They're chocolate chip, your favorite," she said beaming.

"Yummy, thank you so much," Sam said smiling and reached down and picked her up giving her a big bear hug.

"Sammy ate the one that he was saving. I told him not to, but he wouldn't listen," Cassie said in a disapproving look.

"It's okay, one is enough for me," Sam said

putting her down and patting Sammy on his head.

"I really tried daddy," Sammy said looking up with a guilty look.

"I know son, thank you for thinking of me, it's the thought that counts," Sam said trying to comfort him.

Then turning his attention to his wife, "how was your day babe?"

"Good," Jacquelyn replied stepping closer hugging him with a quick kiss.

"Hmm, that bad huh?"

"Just long and stressful, I'll tell you about it later. Now who's ready for dinner?" Jacquelyn asked her voice sounding brighter.

Sam always loved the way she could put away the stress of the day and not let it dominate family time.

"Instead of cooking tonight babe, why don't we order pizza?"

This was immediately followed by the kids begging. "Please mommy, please mommy."

"Well…" Jacquelyn paused, "okay, pizza it is."

"Don't forget to get my favorite mommy," Cassie said making sure she would get her own special veggie pizza.

"I won't darling," Jacquelyn told her smiling.

"Now what about daddy and Sammy, regular?" Which meant meat lovers.

"Sounds great hun," Sam said with Sammy nodding his head yes in agreement. "I'll pick it up babe if you'll call it in."

"Deal," she said already pulling her smartphone out of her pocket. "Twenty minutes babe," she said putting her phone away.

"Okay I'll get ready to go," Sam said and walked into the kitchen to get his wallet and keys he always kept in the top drawer. Then returned to the living room and whispered, "pizza picnic," in Jacquelyn's ear. She nodded and smiled. The kids loved having them, since they were reserved for special occasions. He knew they would be thrilled.

"Guess what kids?" Jacquelyn spoke up.

"What?" They asked.

"Daddy says we are going to have a pizza picnic!" She told them smiling at the looks of surprise on their faces. Cassie and Sammy started jumping up and down squealing.

"But, on one condition," Jacquelyn said frowning. Both children stopped.

"What? Anything," Cassie pleaded.

"Yeah, what mommy," Sammy chimed in.

Sam had to stop himself from laughing out loud.

"The condition is… you have to help me set up for the picnic," she told them.

"Oh yes mommy. Can I put the blanket down?" Cassie asked.

"Of course honey."

"Can I put the plates out," Sammy asked.

"Sure honey," Jacquelyn answered.

"I better get going so our pizzas don't get cold," Sam said and kissed Jacquelyn and headed out.

"That was so wonderful of you Sam," Alana's voice startled him as he neared his truck.

"Sorry."

"Not your fault, sometimes I forget you're around," Sam said climbing into his truck.

"You have a great family," Alana said softly.

"They are," Sam said in a flat tone.

"Does that trouble you?"

"Just never want them to find out what I'm doing."

"Worry not my darling," Alana's voice turning musical.

"Easy for you to say, you can't be arrested," Sam retorted.

"True, but I have ways of concealing our actions."

"Good because we may need it if something goes wrong."

"We will succeed and vengeance will be ours," Alana purred.

"We, I thought this was about me getting justice for my sister's murder?"

"When Marlena summoned me, it was for you, for your vengeance; my fate became intermingled with yours the instant I stepped back into this realm," she explained.

"And I am eternally grateful for all your help," Sam told her warmly.

"You're very welcome darling," Alana told him as they were pulling into the driveway with the pizzas.

As he stepped through the front door Alana whispered, "see you later darling." He nodded and was greeted by the kids and Jacquelyn.

"Oh it smells great, thanks daddy," Cassie said taking the top box.

"Careful darling," Sam told her gently.

"I'm a big girl, look I helped mommy set up the picnic," Cassie said proudly.

"Looks wonderful," Sam said looking at the blanket spread out on the living room floor complete with cups; plates, silverware, and drinks.

They all sat around in a circle around the pizza and dug in when Cassie asked, "Is this a special day daddy? We only have pizza picnics on special days."

"Yes darling we are celebrating being a family and we love each other," Sam said smiling.

Cassie's brow furrowed a little as she took another bite of pizza.

"Can we have special night every day?" she asked excited.

"If we had them every day, they wouldn't be special, would they? But we'll have them more often, how's that?" Sam told her smiling.

"Yay," Cassie cheered.

Sammy was too engrossed in his pizza to chime in.

The emotional turmoil began to stir within him, slowly at first, steadily building into an uncontrollable crescendo of competing anger, hate, rage, and the pure ecstasy of anticipation of the night's coming events. The rush of thoughts, of unleashing his demons to slake his thirst for blood; the blood of the murderous bastards responsible for his pain, his loss.

"Darling are you okay?" Jacquelyn asked him when she saw his expression change.

He snapped out of his thoughts back to reality. "I'm fine babe, just passing thoughts," he said dismissing her concern.

"Have you taken your medicine today?"

"Of course," he lied. He had been secretly been flushing it down the toilet and now felt more alive than ever. His mind was clear and sharp; though at times his thoughts raced so fast he had a hard time keeping up with them. It was worth it, he hadn't felt this good in years. Now nothing would stand in his way of getting revenge, not even Jacquelyn. Part of him was angry at her for keeping him on his medicine, yet he knew deep down that she was only trying to protect him, give him time to heal. But were his parents and his wife trying to control him? Why were they denying him his past? It had been ten years; wasn't that long enough?

The emotional turmoil was overwhelming making him enraged, yet he hid it, he could not be who he wanted to be. He wasn't a monster, or evil, he was simply driven to do what was necessary, what others wouldn't or couldn't do. He would make sure no one would stand in his way, justice would be done. He wondered if it was evil for him to receive pleasure from killing those responsible for murder. Was he playing God? The answers would have to wait, now was the time for action, time for vengeance, time to seek retribution for their murderous deeds they have committed. Tonight another would meet their fate by his hands.

Thankfully the rest of the evening went well;

Jacquelyn busied herself with the kids and cleaning up. After she got them ready for bed he went to their rooms and kissed them goodnight like so many times before. Sam cherished everything about his kids.

"Coming to bed dear?" Jacquelyn asked as she walked down the hallway.

"Not yet, I'm going to go over some proposals for an upcoming project we're bidding on. If we get it, it will be the largest job we've ever had. I know dad is going to need all the help I can give him."

"Just don't overdo it," Jacquelyn said in her motherly tone.

"I won't babe," Sam said smiling.

"I know you darling, once you get going on something you get obsessed and push yourself to the limit."

"I know babe, I'll try not to, taking this time off has made me feel like a new man," Sam smiled.

"I'm glad honey," she said giving him a warm hug and kiss.

"See you in the morning babe, love you," Jacquelyn said as she went into the bedroom.

"Night babe, love you too," he replied.

"It's nice to see love and compassion," a ghostly musical voice spoke behind him, slightly startling him before he realized it was Alana.

"I love them so much, I hope they know that," Sam said softly.

"I'm sure they do darling, you are a great father and husband. Your family is very fortunate and blessed to have a man like you."

"I don't know about that, I try to be good to them."

"You are darling; if you were not a good man I would not have come to aid you in your quest to avenge your sister's murder."

"Thank you Alana," Sam said with a hint of a smile playing at his lips.

"No thanks necessary, you are worthy of my assistance. Throughout the centuries I've helped many, however you are special. It is you who have been chosen for a higher purpose one of a select few. You will succeed where others have failed, it is your fate."

"Let's hope you're right," Sam said grinding his teeth together impatiently.

"Easy darling, I know you're anxious to deal with Kingston, don't worry his death will come tonight I promise," Alana reassured him.

Her words gave him a quiet courage and hope he needed to know he was doing the right thing, and helped him to understand why.

Sam walked over and sat down on the living room couch.

"Are you okay my love."

"I'm fine, just a memory came through of my sister. Why did you call me, 'my love'?" Sam asked trying to change the subject because his head was starting to throb.

"I'm sorry darling, it's an old habit. I won't use that term again if you don't want me too," Alana said shyly.

"No…no it's fine, it's just…nothing," Sam stumbled his words.

"Darling you can tell me anything, after all we are in this together," Alana's voice filled with fiery passion.

"I've heard someone call me that before, but it seems like it was a different place and time, strange I know," Sam said unsure if it wasn't the result of a past dream.

"Not at all my love, our spirit lives many lifetimes on earth."

"You mean reincarnation?"

"Yes, but not as it is taught by many religions; our spirit cannot leave this earth until we overcome certain things. We are sent back until we do and once we overcome evil, the spirit can cross over into heaven and go no more out," Alana explained.

"What happens when people choose evil over and over?"

"Depends, if the spirit of the person is truly evil it is sent to the fiery abyss, never to return."

"Let's hope we can send Kingston there tonight," Sam gritted his teeth feeling the upwelling anger rising inside him.

"We will my darling," Alana's smiling face glowed with a soft golden hue.

"Jacquelyn should be asleep by now," Sam said making sure his voice wasn't too loud.

"Let's go," he said, trying to mask the excitement rising in him, adrenaline surging through his veins once again.

"Very well my love."

"I like that."

"What?"

"You calling me 'love' it feels so natural," Sam said tenderly.

Alana's form shimmered with a silvery light.

"Ah my darling Sam it is an honor and pleasure to aid you in your quest for justice," Alana said with a seductive tone in her voice.

"You are too kind Alana, without you I wouldn't have remembered my sister, which my family was intent on keeping my memories locked away from me, nor would I be able to avenge her."

"Don't worry my love soon you will be whole

again. We have help from on High; we will succeed were others have failed. Nothing will stop us," Alana's said in a firm voice.

"We'll find out."

"Do you think it is safe to leave now?"

"Should be, Jacquelyn's sleeping medicine should have taken effect by now and the kids are asleep, they sleep well through the night now," Sam said.

"Remember don't underestimate Kingston, he's very powerful, one mistake is all it takes," Alana said gravely.

"I will be careful," Sam reassured her.

"Let's go," Alana said in that light musical tone as if they were going out to a carnival.

Sam let the truck roll back out of the driveway into the street before starting it. He wanted to make sure not to wake anyone up.

"So which way are we going?"

"Go south on Main Street and head towards the riverfront. There's an old industrial complex where he lives next to it."

"Okay," Sam replied turning onto Main Street.

"He may be waiting for us, he knows Demarkov and Carlson are dead by now and will be expecting the same fate. He doesn't know who we are so that should give us a little advantage."

"He will pay as the others have," Sam spoke firmly with the conviction of a man driven by fierce love; love for his family, love for what is right, love of justice. Could it be the love of killing? He had to believe the last part wasn't true. He was better than that, he would not allow the demons to win, and he would rather die than become evil.

Alana could see the different emotions washing over Sam's face. "My love, rest your mind and worry not, you are safe from evil, you are chosen and help is by your side. I see your mind and your soul, they are righteous and just," Alana said with heartfelt warmth.

"Thank you for helping me see the truth and giving me strength to do what is right," Sam said as he turned off Main Street towards the waterfront district, parts of which were being revitalized, small shops lined the upper part with red brick streets and picnic areas. He turned down towards the bad end where old industrial complexes still stood in silent testament to the once booming manufacturing heart of the city, now a crumbling reminder of a by-gone era.

"Just ahead," Alana's voice snapped him out of his reverie.

"There, the small blue house at the end of the building," she directed.

Sam pulled over and parked just before the house, he didn't want to alert Kingston.

"Here we go," Sam said out loud as if

reassuring himself of what he was about to do.

He quietly got out of his truck, scanning the entire area to make sure no one was around; there wasn't. This time of the year few ventured out after dark, content to be indoors protected from the harsh elements.

Sam walked towards the house stopping a short distance from it and scanned the surroundings once more. No movement, just distant sounds of a night time city. He took a few more steps and paused, he could hear something, yet couldn't tell what direction it was coming from. Thanks to a grenade exploding close to his left side, his left ear had been badly damaged and now he had a hard time being able to tell what direction a sound was coming from.

"It's okay darling, it's just sounds coming from the river," Alana assured him.

Sam watched a moment longer before approaching the front of the blue house. "Is he home?" Sam asked in a hushed tone.

"Yes, he's in his sanctum," Alana answered.

Sam walked up to the front door, it was locked of course. However he came prepared with a small crowbar. With a quick pop the front door opened. He paused making sure Kingston hadn't heard him and come charging out.

"We're good," he whispered.

Sam was as tense as a coiled viper ready to

strike at an instant. He looked at the front room it was painted an aqua blue color that seemed to shimmer like the ocean. It was sparsely furnished with a couch; chair two end tables with lamps, and a coffee table all in the same aqua blue color. The lamps were emitting a soft bluish white light which lent to the effect of the room. It was nauseating as if one were on a small ship in the middle of the ocean.

"Don't let the effect get to you Sam, it's meant to disorient anyone who enters."

"It certainly works, my head is spinning," Sam said shaking his head to rid the effect.

"Look at the floor, don't look at the walls, focus on the door at the end of the room. It leads to the sanctum. He's down there now preparing his next victim."

"Let's hurry then; maybe we can save them," Sam told Alana his heart racing, all his thoughts on saving whomever Kingston had in his clutches.

He walked slowly to the door and turned the knob and opened it as quietly as he possibly could, trying not to make a sound. A stairwell led downward, he could the muffled sounds of a woman in distress mixed with a man's voice saying something he couldn't understand.

"He's nearly finished with the ritual," Alana alerted Sam.

He hurried down the stairs quickly using the element of surprise to charge Kingston like a lion pouncing on its prey. Kingston was caught completely off guard as Sam slammed into his midsection like a football player tackling an opponent. Sam's charge was so powerful it took Kingston off his feet and sent both them crashing into the wall. Kingston let out a howl of pain as Sam's shoulder pinned his midsection to the wall knocking the wind out of him. Yet Kingston was no push over, he slammed both of his locked fists down hard on Sam's back knocking him to the floor.

"You son-of-a-bitch," Kingston yelled in rage. "You think you can come into my sanctum and attack me! YOU FOOL!" Kingston vehemently spat right before kicking Sam in the head.

Sam's world spun out of control in a mix of blackness and swirling lights, yet somehow he managed to back away to gain a few precious seconds to regain his bearings. Kingston was much stronger than the others Sam thought as Kingston charged at him when suddenly a silvery round disk of swirling energy appeared in front of him and caused Kingston to bounce off send him careening backwards across the room.

"Are you okay my love?" Alana asked tenderly.

"I will be," Sam replied through the biting pain in his head.

"You charged off into the sanctum before I could break the runes and enter," she scolded him.

"I'll remember that the next time," Sam said

rubbing his forehead trying to ease the throbbing pain setting in.

"Okay let's finish this," Sam grinned as he headed back at Kingston.

"You can't stop us, no one can," Kingston's words filled with contempt.

"Wanna bet?" Sam said looking him straight in his eyes and seeing the all-consuming evil radiating from them, enraging him even more. Everything went black for a second and when he came too, he was choking the life out of Kingston.

"No darling, not here, wait," Alana said urgently pleading with him, snapping him out of his rage.

Sam's grip loosened from Kingston's neck leaving his limp body crumpled on the floor.

"Hurry, bind him," Alana directed.

Sam pulled the zip ties he had brought and bound his hands and feet; again he heard the moans of a woman close by.

He looked over and saw a young woman tied to a wide board above a large tank of water which looked like a huge aquarium. Sam climbed on top of the altar and untied the woman causing her to roll into the large tank and caused her to shriek in terror.

"It's okay!" Sam jumped into the tank which only came to his waist and took the woman's shaking hands into his warm strong ones looking her in the eyes.

"It's okay, you're okay now, you are going to be fine," Sam assured her.

She flung her arms around him, "thank you, thank you for saving me," she sobbed.

"Here, let's get you down," Sam said gently and moved to the end of the tank where there was a platform and steps leading down.

"I have a cell phone in my truck, but I must ask you to do something for me," Sam told her.

"My name is Emily," she said.

"I am Sam," he replied.

"Thank you Sam you save me," she said through tear stained eyes. Sam hugged her warmly doing his best to console her.

"I'm going to take Kingston with me and he will never hurt anyone again," he assured her.

"However I must ask you to never reveal anything about me to the police," Sam ask her holding her close to assure her of her safety. He had been in the situations before in the lives of innocent civilians in his arms shell-shocked by the atrocities committed by their own countrymen.

"I promise Sam, I will never say anything about you to anyone."

"Let's get you out of here. I have a blanket in the truck. I'll go get it and the cell phone."

He walked over to Kingston and picked him up and put him on his shoulders and headed up the stairs. Sam soon returned with the cell phone and blanket. He wrapped the blanket around her shivering body, she was so small so innocent Sam thought no one deserves this.

"Now come with me upstairs," Sam told her as she followed him up to the front room.

"I need a favor from you."

"Anything," she said breathlessly.

"Wait five minutes after I leave and call 911and tell them where you are."

"I don't know where I'm at," she cut in.

"You're at 1050 Water St. on the riverfront, as soon as you call them and give them the address, please throw the phone into the river," Sam instructed her carefully.

"You save my life, anything for you," Emily said firmly, committed to honor the man who rescued her.

Sam placed his hand on her cheek, "you're going to be fine."

"Thank you," she said tearing up again grabbing him and hugging him tightly.

"Just remember what I told you. I must go now and finish when I came here to do," Sam said and headed for his truck. Alana's form reappeared as soon as he shut his door

"Do you think she will do as I ask?" Sam ask Alana as he started the truck and headed down the dark street.

"I do, she will be ever thankful for your help," Alana said.

"Our help," you mean Sam corrected, Alana smiled broadly

"My darling we are a great team, Alana spoke in that seductive musical tone that Sam loved.

Chapter 13 Voodoo and Alchemy

"Hello Sarah," Dr. Vorgol said warmly as if meeting an old friend. This irked Colburn.

"Hello Dr. Vorgol, it's great to see you. I'm sorry it's been so long. Work has been draining all my time," Sarah said and then introduced James.

"This is my partner Detective Colburn, and James this is Dr. Vorgol."

"Welcome both of you, come in and have a seat," Dr. Vorgol said waving to the nearby chairs. Coburn and Breckenridge sat down.

"May I offer you something to drink, coffee, or perhaps something a little stronger? He asked warmly like overly sweet candy that would make you sick if you eat too much. Colburn didn't like him; he couldn't put a finger on it, just a gut feeling. Breckenridge was completely taken in by him, which also pissed him off. When he looked up he didn't realize that both Breckenridge in the professor were staring at him.

"Sorry what were you asking?" Once he realized he had asked him a question.

"The professor was asking you if you had seen anything like this in the past that you would've considered related." Sarah repeated the question clearly agitated by his lack of attention.

"Once when I was working vice there was a prostitute murdered close to the campus. The victim had a strange symbol carved into her chest. It is still a cold case, they were never any suspects and we could not connect it to anyone."

"Why haven't you told me those James? Breckenridge was fuming.

"It didn't occur to me until just now, after all there was nothing before or after," Coburn said defensively.

"That you have failed to find and now we have bodies popping up everywhere. I want the case file as soon as we get back to the precinct."

"Yes ma'am," Coburn snapped sharply.

Breckenridge could see that she made him angry, "sorry James I know it's not your fault."

The professor cleared his throat, "I remember the murder you're speaking of Detective Colburn and I doubt it's related to the current events it sounds like you're dealing with a cult."

This turned both their attention back to the professor, "do you think it's one of the core members who are doing it or one of the families of one of the victims who we found out for revenge?" Sarah ask.

"Someone with a motive for revenge is going to extraordinary measures to publicize their work," Vorgol spoke slowly as of guarding his words not wanting to go to the wild theories.

"Doctor do you think we will see much more

of the same style killings," Coburn ask.

"If the person thinks he has got the ones responsible he won't continue killing."

"What makes you think it's a man?" Colburn asked suspiciously.

"Just based on what I've picked up from the news. The two presumed murders were cremations with a note. It wouldn't occur to me that a woman would go through the lengthy process of cremation and placing the ashes directly outside of a police station. So it is logically a man who is trying to make a statement about society. That's why I also don't think it's one of the cult's members'. Usually when a cult comes to the end and is no longer active, the members will disperse or possibly even commit suicide. So naturally that is led me to a conclusion that we are dealing with a vendetta killer."

"What size cult do you think we could be dealing with?" Breckenridge ask.

"Based on what you've told me I could imagine no more than five. I looked over some of the pictures you emailed me. They are blending several different belief systems like voodoo and alchemy yet I saw symbols that came from the Babylonians and Samaria."

"Is that why you feel we are not dealing with many people involved in this cult?" Colburn ask.

"Normally most cults contain a central belief system and will twist a religion to fit their true desire. For example Christianity there have been a multitude of charismatic people who have led groups of people to their own death."

"Can you give us an estimate of how many people we may be dealing with?" Breckenridge ask.

"In my opinion again not more than five unless they have small covens in other places. Would you look at the time; I have another class starting in twenty minutes."

"That's okay we have to go this case is developing so fast I can barely keep up," Sarah said.

"If anyone can, you can," Vorgol smiled.

"Thanks," Breckenridge smiled.

Colburn don't like them being all chummy as a matter of fact he even felt a twinge of jealousy. Sarah was someone he wanted and didn't want anyone to get in the way. Yet he wasn't sure if she felt the same way. He couldn't openly ask her out because someone in the department might find out. They were no way in hell they will be allowed to work together and God help him if he made enemies with her father the mayor.

"James... James," Sarah repeated louder. "What's going on you've been quiet since we've left?" Breckenridge ask getting into her unmarked cruiser.

"Nothing," he said dismissively.

"Nothing my ass, look I need you to be sharp. I can't do this on my own they are too much information coming too fast. If you can't handle it let me know and I'll get another partner," Breckenridge said flatly.

"What, no I'm fine I was just making sure I didn't miss anything between you and Dr. Vorgol. I wanted to make sure I understood what we're up against."

"Now I see."

"See what?"

"You're jealous."

"Jealous of what?"

"I know you like me; I see it every time you look at me. Remember I'm a detective not some silly college girl, besides they will never anything between me and him I took a few classes from him and we share the same passion for religion."

James let out a sigh of relief, "well to be honest I am interested in you," James said mildly, "but we're partners and your dad's the mayor I'd be lucky not to be busted down to a meter maid," James sighed.

"Don't worry we haven't done anything wrong, yet."

James laughed causing Sarah to laugh as well.

"Let's just get through this case and see where it will go. We have to have our heads clear and be able to focus or we'll never get ahead of our suspect and stop the killings or worse get ourselves killed trying."

"You're right, I promise I will not be a distraction or try to wine and dine you until after; okay."

"Deal," Sara Smiled.

"What's our next move?"

"I've asked for the FBI to be brought in, they are sending special investigators and a profiler who will make up a psychological profile of our suspect and help us determine if they are more than one. Initially four agents are available. We need all the help we can get,"

"Agreed," Coburn said nodding his head yes.

"Why are you so few words?"

"Huh," Colburn replied.

"You seem lost in thought and I'm not a mind reader. So tell me what's going on in your mind."

"Nothing is making sense as far as having a family member of one of the victims being our killer. And serial killers almost always work alone. I can understand if we had one serial killer who was murdered by someone who found out that he had killed one, but two in a row and on such a short time frame. Besides, once whoever had killed the serial killer responsible; why continue?"

"You're right serial killers often to go decades without being caught and here we already have two. It's unlikely a family member of one of the deceased is our suspect however, at this point we can't rule out. I think we have a better understanding tomorrow once we get a profile from the FBI team."

"I just hope we don't have any more surprises in the morning."

"What do you mean?" Sarah ask, evidently missing what James was talking about.

"Piles of ashes."

"Oh."

"You really get absorbed in your work don't you? You hungry?" James asked, noting that the time was way past 7 p.m.

"Starving."

"I know a little place up here that has the greatest pizza."

"Sounds great just point the way," Sara smiled.

"Left at the next light, then three blocks on the left the place is called Angelo's."

"I know that place too; they make the greatest white cheese pizza in Columbus."

"I love their supreme meat pizza, they actually put whole strips of bacon on it."

"I can't believe we love the same place. It's such a small place, what are the odds?"

"What can I say we both have great taste," James said with a laugh causing Sarah to laugh as well. It wasn't long before they pulled in the parking lot, thankfully they weren't busy. As they approached the door James opened it for her.

"Thank you," she smiled. "I see chivalry isn't dead."

"Not yet," James smiled.

They grabbed the first booth they could find and it took off their jackets and waited for a waiter, which wasn't long.

"What can I get for you tonight?" A plump waitress asked warmly.

James looked at Sarah giving her the chance to order first.

"I'll have two large slices of white cheese pizza and a Diet Pepsi to drink please."

"And I'll have three slices of medium supreme pizza and a Coke to drink please," James ordered.

Once the waitress left James asked; "do you think the FBI profiler will do us any good?"

"They're exceptional at their jobs and can identify characteristics that often go unnoticed by even the best detectives, including myself."

"Don't sell yourself short, I know I don't have a lot of time in the field as a detective, but you are one of the sharpest and most intelligent persons I've ever met."

Sarah blushed and smiled. "Thank you James that's very kind of you. I hope I can live up to your expectations."

"You have and I'm sure you always will."

"I wished I had your confidence," she said as the waitress returned with the drinks and food which smelled so good.

"Let's dig in."

"You bet."

"I was wondering what your thoughts were about the day's events?"

"Well to be honest, it's a little overwhelming; contending with a second murder and the discovery of a mass grave we're more victims were found."

"How many bodies have been recovered so far?"

"Four and possibly more to come, let's hope they're there no more," Sarah said grimly.

"Do you think they are tied to the Vendetta killer?"

"I can't see the Vendetta killer involved in these murders it doesn't fit his M.O."

"Maybe he's trying to make amends for something he done in his past."

"That makes more sense than a family member of one of the victims getting revenge."

"Whoever it is, they are doing one hell of a job covering their tracks."

"So far they are, but they always make a mistake and leave evidence behind; some small clue that will lead us to them. We have to relentlessly pursue every lead we can."

"Hopefully something will pan out with the funeral homes and the furnace checking."

"Maybe but I'm not counting on it, our suspect knows them well enough to be able to cremate his victims. Just about anyone can, all he needs is access to an out-of-the-way place where he can use a high temperature accelerant. Based on what we know so far we must cover all our bases."

"We should be looking into firefighters who may have had disciplinary action taken against him in the past."

"James that is a great idea after all who knows fire better; first thing in the morning I'll have a couple of detectives check out personnel records of fire departments. It will take a couple of days but it's an avenue we need to follow," Sarah told him.

James felt good that Sarah took his ideals seriously and didn't dismiss him like Captain Harris.

"Hopefully CSU will have more information tomorrow and we will get a solid lead on identifying a suspect," Sarah said as the waitress cleaned away their plates.

James reached for his wallet without thought. "No no, I'll get it," Sarah said.

"No I got this, my treat, you can get the next one," James said as they got up and walked to the car in silence. It was half way back to the station before Sarah broke the silence. "Let's go over what we have so far tonight if you are up for a few more hours works?" Sarah asked.

"I am."

"Good as soon as we get back to the station I would like to go over Carlson's and Demarkov's history to see if we can make any connection between the two there must be something. Then maybe we can find out why they were killed and if by the same suspect. My gut tells me we are dealing with one murderer."

"I agree; for one thing its way to bazaar not to be connected," James agreed.

It wasn't long before they found themselves back at Coburn's desk in the station, which was practically deserted other than a couple of vice cops working the night shift.

On the whiteboard they had pictures of Carlson and Demarkov at the top with black lines drawn between them. At the main top a question mark inside a box representing the unknown suspect and the other line straight down represents possible victims of theirs.

Sarah starred at the board, "we have potential serial killers who were murdered by?" She let the question linger and allowed James to put his opinion.

"There has to be someone who knew both of them and what they did in their past. In the letter the Vendetta Killer left, he told us where to find the bodies of the victims of Carlson and Demarkov. I think it could be some kind of internal struggle for power in whatever cult they belong to, or a vigilante who's done his homework. And if that's the case our suspect would have to have extensive resources and ways of getting information from the justice system. It's easiest way to track people down."

"You bring up some great points. We also need to run an internal search to see if any Carlson's and Demarkov's pop-up. Our killer may be using the web as well. Nowadays you can find just about anyone on social media."

"I thought you would ask that so I ran a search and neither Carlson nor Demarkov was on any social media site and didn't turn up in a general search either."

"Good work; well that's one less thing we'll have to do. I wish forensics would have found something that would have helped us."

"Maybe we're looking at this all wrong, let's look at it in a different way; what's not here? Whoever this is, he was able to subdue two men. At Demarkov's house we know there was a struggle, so we are looking for someone with training. He cleaned the crime scene so we couldn't find any usable DNA or fingerprints. He's also very smart about cremating the bodies so that we cannot determine a cause of death or even if he used a weapon. And he's taunting us with notes and placing the ashes outside of a police station, which says he's better than us. He's playing judge; jury, and executioner. We may be dealing with someone who had military training. That would explain his ability to overpower his victims. However I can't see why he would be in a cult with people like Carlson and Demarkov."

"Maybe he didn't know it at first and found out later and decided to take matters into his own hands. A lot of veterans came back from the Middle East with post-traumatic stress disorder, maybe he snapped."

"Whoever it is has inside knowledge of the cult, coven, or whatever we're dealing with. This guy also has an easy way to find out what these guys were up to and their past."

"My money is on a cult member."

"I'll go with an outsider that is familiar with the legal system maybe even a former cop working on old cold cases who stumbled upon them and put two and two together," James said.

"Damn."

"What? Don't like my ideas?" James ask.

"No look at the time, it's two a.m. we better get our asses out of here. We have to be back at seven a.m. to prep for the F.B.I. conference."

"Shit, you're right I didn't realize how late it was. You want me to walk you to your car?"

"Sure."

They walked together through the parking garage. James followed her to her car and opened the door for her after she unlocked it.

"Ever the gentleman."

"Always," James said as Sarah stood by her car door.

"I really enjoy working with you James," Sarah said and reached in and gave him a quick kiss.

"A little something to think about," Sarah said smiling.

James smiled broadly, "it certainly does. Good night, drive safe."

"You too," Sarah said as she backed out and drove away.

By the time James got back to his apartment and showered it was three a.m. He set his alarm, '*not much sleep before I go back up to go to the precinct*' he thought. His mind still clouded by Sarah's kiss and the rest of the day's events, thankfully he was so tired he went to sleep as soon as his head hit the pillow.

The alarm has been going off for five minutes before he woke up and hit the snooze button and drifted back off to sleep for another five minutes before the alarm sounded again. *Okay, okay* he thought as he shut it off and set up in bed scratching his head doing his best to focus.

Damn he thought to himself as he walked to the bathroom and took another shower and brushed his teeth after he shaved. He always liked me to clean the well-groomed especially around Sarah. Although this morning he wasn't feeling it; the case was overwhelming so many facts it was a blur in his mind. So many pictures; statements, CSU reports, forensics, and God knows what the FBI will add to the investigation. And not to mention a mean-ass captain who expects daily reports on Sarah and his crush on her; shit it was all he could do to handle it.

James filled his coffee travel mug up and headed out the door. He wanted to get there early to make sure he had his notes in order. He didn't want to look like a fool in front of the captain or Sarah for that matter. He arrived at the station at a quarter after six.

To his surprise the F.B.I. were already there along with Sarah and the captain. They were all huddled in the captain's office. James felt left out. Why didn't Sarah tell him they were going to meet earlier? He thought as he walked to his desk as they were finishing. As Sarah approached his desk he pretended to be going through the case file.

"Good morning," Sarah said smiling.

"Morning," James said a little less enthusiastically.

"What's wrong," Sarah asked realizing James wasn't acting like his normal self.

"You tell me? Why did you leave me out of this morning's meeting?" James asked sharply.

"I called, check your phone James I didn't leave you out of anything," Sarah said with a tone of anger in her voice.

James checked his phone sure enough he had missed her call. "Sorry," James said put in his head down as if he were in trouble.

"It's okay you didn't miss anything we were just going over what we were going to go over at the seven a.m. meeting."

"I thought…" James started.

"Well quit thinking so damn much. Now let's go compare notes so we don't look like idiots in front of the F.B.I.," Sarah said before the captain called everyone into the small conference room.

"Everyone I have asked the FBI to join our investigation. From now on report all findings to them. Two additional teams are arriving later today due to the complex nature of this case and the rising body count. We no longer have the resources to handle a case of this size. Breckinridge and Colburn will take the lead and liaison with the F.B.I. Detective Meninx will coordinate with the uniformed officers and county and state officials. Now I'll turn it over to special agent Dewall," Captain Harris said.

"Ladies and gentlemen we are here not to take over your case or step on your toes. We are here to help you solve these crimes. Special agent Thompson is the best profiler's we have so she will guide us on what we're looking for in finding our suspect," said agent Dewall.

"Thank you agent Dewall, I have spent last night reviewing the information we have so far on

our suspect and the lack of it. We are having one
of our own CSU units revisit each crime scene to see
if we can find anything that was missed during the
initial investigation. So far our profile is of a white
male, late thirties to early forties possibly with
military training. The person also has an intimate
knowledge of fire and how to use it. So our prime
targets are anyone who may be a firefighter; a
veteran, or a funeral worker who performs
cremations. Remember the guy will not stand out in
public he may even be a family man. We do not
believe he is associated with any cult. He may have
found out about them and taking matters into his own
hands," Agent Thompson told them.

"How does the suspect know about the killers
past?" Coburn ask.
"The unsub may have tortured the first cult member
to get the information about the others. He may have
found out about Carlson by accidentally running
across him someway," said agent Thompson.

"So you think we are dealing with a cult," this
time it was Breckenridge asking the question.

"I believe that is the only option that makes
sense at this point, however let's try to keep an open
mind out there," Thompson said.
Suddenly the captains phone rang he stepped out
quickly to answer it. A few minutes later he walked
back in. All eyes turned to him as the room grew
quite.

"Everyone roll out I want answers," the
captain said. "Colburn, Breckenridge my office
now."

"I know you two can get me the answers I
need. Do what you have to do, but do it faster. And

don't play any fucking games with me, you report
to me before anyone else got it," Captain Harris said.

"Yes Captain," they both said quickly.

"And Breckenridge just because the mayor's
your father doesn't mean shit to me. I was here
before he became mayor and I will be here after. Do
you understand me?" Harris asked. "Now go out
there and catch this son-of-a-bitch!"

Chapter 14 Kingston

It was like coming home again the creaks and groans of the old structure; the dull sounds of his footsteps of the cold damp concrete floor, the hiss of gas burners as they roared to life bringing forth its glorious heat.

"Anything you want to say?" Sam asked, loosening the tightly bound gag around Kingston's mouth which left a deep red indentation.

"I see the Nabila has summoned her again," Kingston said.

"What do you mean?"

"You must take us for fools. We found out about you and your little helper. It's a matter of time before my brothers find her."

"I work alone," Sam ground his teeth together.

"Is that why you have a pet spirit?" Kingston spat.

Sam backhanded him before he knew it.

"Ah did I hurt your feelings!" Kingston gloated.

"We'll see whose feelings get hurt in a minute when you're screaming like a bitch," Sam smiled wildly.

"Darling don't let him anger you," Alana's soothing voice whispered in Sam's ear.

"Does she always tell you what to do?" Kingston asked.

"You and your friends have had this coming for a while and now it's time," Sam answered with a growl to his voice. "But first let's take a little souvenir, shall we?" Sam said pulling out a set of metal shears.

"And you say I'm the sick one," Kingston retorted.

"Don't worry I'll cure you," Sam laughed as he severed Kingston's right thumb and then his left. "What no screaming? He's a tough one Alana."

"Remember my love, don't be overcome by hatred," Alana's voice always calmed him.

"You're right let's be done with it. Any last prayers Kingston?"

"You're no different than me," Kingston said with a twisted grin making Sam angry again, but he stayed in control.

"I do not take innocent lives," Sam rebutted as he hooked the giant metal hook to the bounds that held Kingston's arms together.

"Don't worry you will join your friends soon. What it is you call yourselves; ahh yes 'The Avox'.

Soon there will be no more of you filthy scum to contaminate the earth," Sam spat taking pleasure in announcing his sentence.

"Oh but you're wrong they are more of us than one group," Kingston said mockingly.

"Finish it Sam," Alana's voice came again. "He's trying to buy time. Finish him," her voice came through loud and clear.

Sam raised the chain lifting Kingston into the air.

"I see who the pet is now," Kingston bellowed as Sam raised him over the large iron crucible already glowing from the intense heat of the flames. Soon Kingston would be just a memory, lost in the eons of time.

Still Sam was angry at the idea of being anyone's pet, he was a full grown man and be damned if he would ever cower down and be submissive to anyone.

"Sam," Alana's voice snapped him out of his thoughts and back to the gristly task at hand.

"Darling do not let him play mind games with you, he's just buying time to try and escape," Alana purred.

"No worries my love, he doesn't stand a chance, besides he doesn't understand our relationship," Sam boasted at Kingston.

I don't; do I?" Kingston asked raising an

eyebrow.

Sam lowered Kingston a little so he could look him directly into his eyes.

"You don't!" Sam roared as he raised Kingston back up and moved him over the large rusty iron crucible. This time Sam wasted no time lowering Kingston into the intensely hot kettle. The screams died quickly as soft blue flames gently rolled up and out of the old heavy kettle.

"I'm sorry my love," Sam whispered quietly.

"My darling Sam you have nothing to be sorry for. I know this is hard on you and you should not have to be in this position you're in. Yet together we shall prevail over our enemies."

"Yes we shall," Sam smiled.
"Only two more left," Alana said solemnly.

"And my sister will have justice. We must find her body, she should have a proper burial," Sam said grimly.

"Never worry darling we will find her."
Then it occurred to Sam, "will you leave me after all this is over?" he asked in a gloomy voice.

"If you wish to carry on fighting evil I can stay by your side if you so desire," Alana said warmly.

"I desire it very much," Sam smiled broadly realizing he would continue to have Alana in his life; finally someone who truly understood him. Although he loved Jacquelyn, they were things she wouldn't understand nor would he expect her to.

"Then it is settled; I will stay my love," Alana spoke in that light musical tone she used when she was happy.

"So it is," Sam smiled at the thought of having Alana in his life. Was it crazy he felt so strongly about a spirit? He would worry about that later; right now he had to get the job done. Steam was still rising out of the large iron cubicle. It was taking longer with Kingston than the others.

"Why is he taking longer?" Sam asked.

"His element was water and due to that, his essence was infused with it," Alana answered.

"I see, I'll turn up the heat so we can get done before Jacquelyn wakes up and realizes I'm gone."

The flames roared higher and brighter as Sam turned the gas valve. Steam billowed out of the cauldron before finally dying down.

"Wow," Sam said amazed.

"They have power and that's why we must be careful going after the next two."

"We will," Sam said as he lowered the kettle to check on the progress. "Finally, it's done," Sam said relieved.

He turned off the gas and allowed the old crucible to cool enough to scoop the remains up into a small metal bucket. He had already prepared the type written letter to the police. It wasn't long before he arrived at the police station. It was a different one; going back to the first one would only be asking to get caught.

He piled the ashes up and placed one of Kingston's thumbs on top of the envelope containing the letter and climbed back into his truck. Three a.m. damn he was cutting it close. Jacquelyn normally got up at five thirty or six depending on him and the kids. Thankfully her sleep medicine kept her from waking through the night and would allow him to slip in.

"Now they're only two left," Alana said.

"Good, the sooner the better," Sam said sternly as he drove.

"Don't worry darling, vengeance will be yours. They will pay for what they've done."

"Yes they will as well as others who do the same. We will cleanse this land of evil," Sam smiled.

By the time Sam and Alana got back it was 3:30 am, "whew we are cutting it close."

"Yes we have."

Sam slipped inside quietly and went to the guest bathroom to wash and change into his night clothes. He would lie down on the couch and when Jacquelyn got up he would pretend to have gotten up in the middle of the night hurting and took some medicine and lay down on the couch not wanting to wake her up. He was too wired up to go to sleep.

"Do you really think there are more of them?"

"It's very possible; I will look for them today and fine out while you're at work."

Damn he had forgotten all about work. It was going to be a long day. He didn't mind it too much; at times he would stay up for days and felt fine, even taking the medicine that was suppose to make him sleep. And now that he wasn't taking them he began feeling like his old self again.

"Is the fourth Avox in Columbus?"

"Yes he is close, but Sam he is very powerful and we have to plan to catch him at his weakest. We need to catch him outside of his sanctum where he won't be as strong. Unless you want to wait until I'm full strength?"

"No we can do this, I'm feeling stronger than I have in years."

"Okay, but we need to be cautious and also careful not to get caught by the police who by now will be increasing patrols throughout the city."

"You're right, but we have God on our side and that's all that matters," Sam rebutted and with that Alana stopped her protest.

"Today I will go and monitor Victor and see what his schedule is."

"I have to go into work today to take care of a

few things. I'll be finished around four and then I have to pick up the kids at five. We can get together after that and make our plans."

"Jacquelyn's up," Alana said suddenly. "I'll see you this evening; goodbye for now my love," she said in that seductive voice that Sam loved.

"See you later," Sam replied as Alana's ghostly image shimmered and was gone.

"There you are, I was wondering where you went," Jacquelyn said sleepily.

"Sorry babe I woke up hurting and didn't want to bother you."

"You're no bother; I want you to wake me up from now on. You've been having more of these episodes. We may need to get you back to the doctor for a checkup just to make sure everything is okay."

"Baby I'm fine."

"Sam, please for me and the kids?" Jacquelyn knew his weak spot.

"Okay okay, call today and set up an appointment and I'll go," Sam gave in, bringing a smile to her face.

"Thank you babe. Are you going to be able to go into work today and pickup the kids? Your mom is going to pick them up from school so you can get them after work. If not I can make arrangements to get them after work, I'll be working late."

"No I'm feeling better, I already took my medicine," Sam lied.

"Okay if you say so, but if you over do it I'm going to kick your butt," she said in a stern tone.

"Really now," Sam said grinning getting up off the couch causing her to smile.

"Yes really," she said as Sam closed in grabbing her and giving her a bear hug and then kissing her.

"Mmm we are going to have to finish that tonight," Sam said grabbing her butt.

"Oh yes," Jacquelyn said moving in for another passionate kiss.

"I love you so much Sam. Please take care of yourself. You are all me and the kids have," Jacquelyn said breathlessly.

Hearing her plea tugged at his heart so painfully he felt a moment of remorse mixed with panic of what if he got killed doing what he was doing.

"I promise baby I will do everything I can to take care of myself and be here for you, always and forever."

"And a day," she finished with a smile. That was their little saying they had between them. "I'll go and wake the kids for school," Jacquelyn said turning to go.

"Let me, I don't get to do it very often. They'll get a kick out of it."

"Okay," she said softly as she followed him down the hallway to the children's bedrooms. Sam slowly opened the door to Cassy's room first and walked softly over to her bed. He always loved to see her so peaceful and quiet. He gently stroked her hair, "wake up honey; it's time for school."

Her little eyes fluttered open. "Hi daddy," she said smiling.

"Good morning honey," Sam said smiling too. Jacquelyn stepped into the room and turned the light on, "morning sweetie."

"Hi mommy," Cassy said happily being fully awake. She was always so easy to get up.

"I'll get Sammy babe while you take care of Cassy," Sam told Jacquelyn.

"Okay."

"Now what would you like for breakfast?" Jacquelyn asked Cassy as they headed off to the kitchen while Sam went to wakeup Sammy. He was always harder to wake up than Cassy.

Sam walked over to his bedside and stroked his head, "hey buddy, wake up, it's time for school," he said softly. No response of course.

"Time to get up," Sam said a little louder still stroking his head causing Sammy to finally stir.

"Daddy," he said half asleep.

"Time to get up and get ready for school. Mommy and Cassy are already in the kitchen fixing breakfast," Sam told him knowing it would get him motivated to get him out of bed. Sam stood up and pulled the covers back so he could get up.

"Better tell mommy what you want for breakfast," Sam told him, sending him running down the hallway. He was always eating, skinny as a rail. As long as he was healthy Sam didn't care.

When Sam got to the kitchen Jacquelyn was already getting cereal ready for Sammy.

"Need any help babe?" Sam asked as he poured himself a cup of coffee, he loved it so much he would drink a whole pot a day.

"Could you get the milk and juice out of the fridge while I get Cassy's omelet made?"

"No problem," he answered taking a sip of coffee. He sat his cup down on the counter and got them from the fridge and went ahead and poured juice and milk for the kids. He fixed Sammy's cereal before sitting down with them at the table.

"Here ya go," Sam sat the heaping bowl of cereal in front of him and watched him dig in. Jacquelyn brought Cassy's omelet over and sat it down in front of her, "careful honey, it's hot," she warned and kissed her on the top of her head.

Sam filled his thermoses; he always packed two in case he was out a long time. He hated drinking gas station coffee, nothing worse than old stale coffee, but it was better than nothing.

"Babe you going to eat anything?" Jacquelyn asked.

"I'll pick up something after I drop the kids off at school."

"Here take your medicine in case you need it."

"I'm good, I've already taken this morning's dose," Sam lied.

"Here, now don't argue," Jacquelyn said firmly.

"Okay," he said giving in to her, besides he had more important things to think about, like the upcoming fight with Victor Vorgol.

"Babe I forgot I have to work late today we won the bid for the Cleveland job," Sam remembered.

"Oh honey congratulations!" she gave him a kiss, "you must be thrilled."

"I am, but a little nervous too, this is the biggest job we've ever taken on," Sam said.

"Well I'm sure you will do a great job. I just don't want you to over do it," Jacquelyn said in her motherly tone.

"I won't," Sam smiled and kissed her, "I promise."

"I'll pick up the kids from your mom's after I get off work, that way you won't have to worry about it, she will love the extra time with them," Jacquelyn said.

After the kids ate she took them to get them dressed for school while Sam packed their lunches.

After a few minutes they were done and ready to go. They loved riding in Sam's pickup truck. Sam gave Jacquelyn a quick kiss as he headed out the door with the kids in tow. She heard a, "bye mommy," as the kids ran to Sam's truck.

Once they were buckled in safely he backed out of the driveway and headed up the street to their school. After dropping the kids off he turned to go to the office.

"Hello dear," Alana said sitting beside him. He flinched a little, he still hadn't gotten used to having a spirit around.

"Sorry if I startled you my love," Alana purred.

"I forget having you around sometimes. I'm sure I'll get used to it in time. I've already told Jacquelyn that I had forgotten about the Cleveland job and that I would be working late today so we can plan once I'm finished up at the office which shouldn't take long."

"Sounds wonderful darling."

"Have you found Vorgol?"

"Yes I have, however it's going to be a little tricky to get to him. He's a professor at the university and lives on campus."

"I'll call Jacquelyn and tell her that I have to go up to Cleveland late tonight so I can be there first thing in the morning. That way we won't have to worry about being out all night. It's a weekday so things should settle down fairly early on campus. We'll just have to watch out for any patrols."

"That will be the least of our worries. His lair is filled with traps to prevent anyone flesh or spirit to enter the sanctum."

"I'm sure we can get past them, after all I've been through worse avoiding improvised explosive devices in Iraq."

"These traps are different Sam they are designed to kill the body and trap the soul. Victor is a very dangerous opponent, that's why he has been so successful over the years."

"His time is up," Sam said grinding his teeth as he pulled into the office. "I'll go and meet with my father so we can finalize the plans for the Cleveland job."

"I'll be close."

Now that he had Victor on his mind Sam found it nearly impossible to concentrate as he headed into the office.

"Sam; you with us?" Richard asked gently tapping him on the shoulder.

"Yeah, sorry I was just thinking about the plans for the job."

"We are taking the earth moving equipment up today and the cranes tomorrow," Richard said.

"What's the time on phase one completion?"

"We should have the ground prepared in four weeks. All the permits are in and we should be able to start phase two of the foundation work after that," Richard answered.

"If we can get a secondary staging area it would help us with a place to store the building supplies. That way we can use the primary staging area for equipment only."

"I think there may be an area a few blocks up from the main site. I'll check on it today and see if we can lease it."

"I can go up first thing tomorrow morning and make sure the equipment arrives safely if you can go up today and lay out the primary staging area," Sam told his father. *Guess I won't have to lie to Jacquelyn*, Sam thought.

"We're also going to have to hire some local labor up there so we can stay on schedule."

"I'll get Jim to check with a couple of temp agencies around Cleveland," Sam said knowing that Jim was the best foreman he had and could be trusted to do the hiring and firing if need be.

"Sounds like we have a good plan, if we get

this job done right and on time it will change our company and double our size," Richard said smiling.

"Don't worry dad we will," Sam said confidently. One thing Sam prided himself on was making his father proud of him. He would walk through the fires of Hell itself. Nothing would stand in his way, he would move heaven and earth if he had to.

"I'll take care of things here while you go to Cleveland."

"Sounds great, I'll call you later with updates."

"Okay, be safe," Sam said giving his dad a quick hug.

"You okay?"

"Yeah, why?"

"Nothing, just making sure you don't overdo it, that's all."

"I won't, love you," Sam told him as he headed out the door and to the yard to find Jim. Which he was usually at the foreman's trailer, god Sam couldn't wait until the day was over. All he could think of was killing Victor Vorgol. That bastard would pay with his life tonight and nothing would stop it.

"Don't let your rage consume you my love," Alana whispered in Sam's right ear.

"I won't my, it's hard, but we will prevail,"

Sam said under his breath standing in front of the foreman's trailer. He walked up the steps and opened the door. Jim was nowhere to be found, but he knew how to find him easy enough. Sam grabbed one of the radios off its charger.

"Jim this is Sam, you copy?" Sam spoke into the radio.

"Go for Jim," Jim's voice came over loud and clear.

"I need you to come over to the trailer, I have some things to go over with you," Sam said.

"Roger, I'll be there in five," Jim responded.

It was Sam's idea to make sure everyone had a two-way radio to make it easy to communicate anytime anywhere on the job. The radios also worked on cellular networks to make sure no one was out of reach. Sam had learned the value of communication in the Army. After a few minutes Jim showed up.

"How you doing?"

"I'm doing good, how have you been?"

"I'm good, it's good to have you back."

"Just had to unwind a little, felt good to take some time off."

"So about the Cleveland job" Jim said getting back on topic he knew Sam was sensitive about his health.

"We are taking the earth moving equipment up

today. I want to make sure that each piece gets a full safety inspection before they're operated. Also I want the cranes gone over with a fine tooth comb, no excuses," Sam told him.

"Sure thing, I'll have everything inspected as soon as I get to the primary staging area. Any particular reason why? They were inspected when we pulled off the last job," Jim asked.

"I have a feeling that we are due for a random OSHA inspection and I don't want to get caught with our pants down, besides we can't be too safe. The last job put a lot of strain on our cranes doing the heavy lifting. Be sure to check for stress fractures on the crane's boom and replace any worn cables if needed," Sam instructed.

"Got it boss; anything else?"

"That should do it. I know it's a lot, but we have a lot riding on this job and can't afford any screw-ups. Also I going to need you to check with a couple temp agencies up there and see if we can get some people for general labor duties. I will have one of the secretaries help you, but you will have me meet them. I want good people Jim and they may be able to come to work full time if this project goes well."

Jim was one of Stout Construction's oldest employees and was on site when Sam's accident occurred. So he knew the importance of safety. He even created the procedure they now use to shut down in windy conditions. They place six wind gauges around the perimeter of the job and once the wind reaches a certain speed it triggers an alarm inside the crane's cab for the operator to shut down.

Once Sam finished up with Jim, he took a walk around the yard looking at various pieces of equipment. He always made it a point to keep it organized and trash free. Stout Construction was one of the best and most efficient companies in Ohio.

He felt Alana's presence near him.

"I was wondering where you went to."

"Just waiting until you were alone. We need to visit Marlena. I must be at my strongest and you must be too for the fight tonight."

"I'm finished here, let's go."

Once they were in his truck he asked, "Why do we need to go to Marlena's?"

"We need her blessings before tonight, they will help protect us from the wards that Victor has set."

"Ward?" Sam asked.

"A ward is like a trap, but created be placing a special symbol that is inscribed with runes to prevent others from passing or inflict grave damage."

"I see," Sam said flatly as he started his truck.

"Don't worry nothing will stop us from getting justice," Alana purred.

"I know," Sam said clenching his jaws

grinding his teeth.

Chapter 15 Psychics

"Damn he is serious about this case," James said under his breath to Sarah not wanting Captain Harris to hear as they left his office into the main area. We have to start canvassing all the psychic and spiritualist places around the city; surely one of them will have a lead we can follow because right now all we have is a profile and that's next to nothing working a complex case like this."

"I'll get as many uniform officers as I can get to hit the streets, later. Can you get a working list together?"

"No problem."

"Right now we have to go to the ME's office. I want to see if they have uncovered anything new."

"Lead the way."

After a few steps she made an abrupt turn

around and nearly ran into him. "Sorry," she said placing her hands on his chest to steady herself. She was so close it was intoxicating. He grabbed her arms to hold her stable when all he wanted to do was hold her and passionately kiss her.

"There you go; you okay?"

"Yes sorry about that I forgot my case file on my desk."

"Oh," James murmured.

She went and got her case and they were off to the ME's office. They walked in silence each absorbed in their own thoughts.

"Hello Dr. Daniels."

"Hello Detective Breckenridge and Detective Colburn," Dr. Daniels greeted them.

"So are there any additional facts about the remains of Demarkov?" Sarah ask.

"No they were identical with the exception of the thumbs and weight."

"Can you tell anything for the state of rigor mortis or rate of decay from the thumbs?"

"I see you are familiar with my field of work," Daniels said smiling. "I rarely run into many cops that know much about it. In the case of the thumbs they were cut off while the victims were alive and show no noticeable decay, so they must have been killed within twenty-four hours of you finding them.

The state of rigor mortis also wasn't advanced enough to indicate otherwise either. Your killer is moving extremely fast from what I can tell. I've never seen anything like it in my entire career as medical examiner."

"Thank you doctor for all your hard work, I'm sure it's going to pay off. Is there anything else you can determine from the remains?"

"Actually I'm glad you ask. There is something unusual about them, although they share the same basic elements, they are some differences between them."

"What do you mean 'different'?"

"When I done the analysis of Carlson's I noticed they were higher than normal concentration of; calcium, magnesium, sodium, and potassium."

"That's the base components of any human remains."

"Yes, but in Carlson's ashes the ratios were elevated extremely high."

"So he was a vitamin junkie."

"Maybe, but…," Daniels started to say.

"But what?"

"They match the profile of what top soil is made of."

"So you're telling me he ingested dirt?"

"If he suffered from Pica he could have."

"Isn't that were people will eat all kinds of weird stuff?" James ask.

"Yes," Daniels answered.

"What about Demarkov?" Sarah ask.

"His actually contained high amounts brimstone."

"You mean sulfur?"

"Yes so much so that it should have killed him."

"That's interesting," Sarah said starring off into space pondering what this information meant.

"This case just keeps getting stranger and stranger," James said breaking the ominous silence.

"Yes it does," Sarah agreed coming back out of her thoughts. "If the timeline holds true there should be another set of ashes at one of our precincts."

"Thankfully they weren't at ours. The Captain would have a full coronary," James said.

Sarah's phone rang.

"Oh shit, I spoke too soon," James said.

"Hello, this is Det. Breckenridge, Sarah answered.

"Yes… we're on our way," she said hanging

up. "Come one James they've been another."

"Where?"

"Thirteenth precinct, it was just found. Call CSU and tell them to high tail it over there while I get a hold of the FBI team."

"You got it."

Both were on their phones as they rushed out of the ME's office. They got into Sarah's patrol car. She hit the lights and siren as she floored it out of the parking structure. James was struggling to get his seat belt on.

"CSU is on the way," he said putting his phone in his pocket. "Just don't kill us trying to get there," James told Sarah as she took a turn sideways.

"Don't worry," she said smiling. "What's wrong you afraid of a little speed?" she ask running through a red light.

"Nope, I just value my life. I don't want this to be my last case," James said in a high pitch, doing his best to hang on.

Within minutes they arrived at the thirteenth precinct. They were two uniform officers standing guard and had already taped off the area.

"Who found this?" Sarah ask walking up to them.

"I did, I saw it after our morning's briefing and was told to call you immediately," the officer on the right spoke up. Calvano was his last name.

"Thank you. Has anything been disturbed?"

"Not as far as I know," Calvano answered.

Breckenridge and Colburn put on latex gloves and stepped over the police tape.

"It's exactly like the other two that were found at our precinct. A pile of ashes with a letter and a thumb on top of it."

"Calvano I need two more officers out here. I have a feeling the press is going to be all over this."

"Yes ma'am," he responded and went into the precinct can came back with two uniform officers and their Captain.

"Hello Captain, I'm Detective Breckenridge and this is Detective Colburn," Sarah introduced them.

"Good to meet you."

"Do you have any cameras in this area?"

"No, after all this is the front entrance to a police station. We've had no need until now."

It wasn't long before CSU arrived and began processing the scene. They photographed everything before bagging the thumb and ashes. They dusted the envelope and letter before handing it to Breckenridge.

"Nothing we can find, just a plain envelope

and letter inside telling us who the victim was and the ashes look the same as the ones before. The letter says that the victim was Markius Kingston and that he was responsible for the deaths of four women and the attempted murder of a fifth," the CSI officer told her.

"That means that we have a survivor, a witness who may be able to identify our suspect," Sarah said in disbelief.

As soon as she was done talking a uniform officer ran up to her with a note. The survivor called 911 early this morning at two a.m. a young female who stated she had been kidnapped earlier that day and had managed to escape.

"Go over everything here with a fine tooth comb and get it back to the ME's office," Sarah instructed the CSU team.

"Come on James we may have gotten our first break in this case!" Sarah said excitedly, already heading to her cruiser with James behind her.

"Find the number for the fifteenth precinct," Sarah ask.

"Already one step ahead of you," James said with his phone up to ear.

"Hello this is Det. Colburn with the twelfth precinct. You brought a woman in early this morning on a kidnapping call. Is she still there? What? No. What's her address? Got it, okay thanks," James said hanging up.

"She's not there?" Sarah asked James after over hearing the conversation.

"After they took her to the hospital and questioned her, they got her contact information they turned her loose," James said.

"James have her brought to our station so we can speak with her and then have her talk to the FBI profiler, also see if they have checked the thumb print to see if Kingston is in the system, also I want them to take DNA from the thumb. See if they can pull a picture of him from the DMV to see if our victim can make a positive ID. Also I want her to meet with a sketch artist to see if she can give us a description of the passerby who let her use their phone. Have one of the uniforms pull the 911 call and see if we can trace that call and find out where it is," Sarah told him as she hit the lights and siren. I want to go by the crime scene first to find out if we can find any clues as to who our unsub is."

James was already on the phone relaying the orders from Sarah.

In no time they were pulling up in front of an old blue house located at the end of an abandon industrial complex. Police and CSI's were swarming the place as they got out of Sarah's cruiser. Agent Thompson, FBI's lead profiler was already there along with four other agents.

"I've never seen anything like this Det. Breckenridge," Agent Thomson said walking up to her as she got out of the car.

"You should see the other two crime scenes," Sarah told him.

"I have, I went to both of them yesterday. We are diffidently dealing with a cult of some type," Thomson said.

"I agree, it just so bizarre it's hard to believe. Things like this are seen in movies," Sarah replied. What did you find inside?"

"You're going to have to see for yourself detectives," Thomson said.

"Okay let's go."

The old house was a single story painted blue which looked past due for a fresh coat of paint. As they walked through the front door the interior walls were painted an aqua blue color that seemed to shimmer. James found it so disorienting it made him want to throw up.

"You okay James?" Sarah ask seeing his discomfort.

"Yeah just a little nauseous that's all."

"Let's go down to the sanctum," Sarah told him.

"Sounds great to me," James said wanting any reason to get out of that room which was making him sick.

"Wow this case just keeps getting more bizarre with every kill."

"We don't know if Markius Kingston is dead."

"Well he is missing a thumb. I just got a text the thumb print is a match for him."

They both went down to the cellar where Kingston preformed his macabre rituals.

"He was the water element killer from the looks of the symbols on the walls and floor, I don't see an altar. It must be the large clear water tank; it's not an aquarium from what I can tell. It looks like he drowns his victims," James concluded.

"I want dive teams and water recovery units here ASAP," Sarah told James who already had his phone out. "The letter stated Kingston had placed the bodies of his victims out from of his house in the Scioto River. I guess he wanted to keep them close, the sick bastard!"

"Did the letter say how many he killed?"

"Four."

"Here take a look at this plumbing at the end of the tank; it looks like he was distilling something."

"I think he was attempting to gather the essence of a person."

"I wouldn't believe you had I not seen the other two crime scenes."

"I want a sample of this water to be tested for DNA. We may be able to match it to some of the victims and tie it to Kingston."

"So you think the other victims were not killed by the vendetta killer?"

"No, I am certain we are dealing with a cult. I just can't figure why all of them are turning up dead. It's one thing to link two different people together to a killer, but three? And not some amateur either; the guy we're dealing with knows what he's doing."

"He'll make a mistake and when he does we will be there to catch him. We are dealing with a highly trained individual who can move many circles, civilian and police. He knows how to erase all evidence of his crimes. Hell if we were to arrest him today we wouldn't be able to prosecute him. No body, no crime. The only thing we have is circumstantial evidence at best."

"I'm impressed James, I underestimated you. That's why we are going to have to catch him in the act. Our best chance now is to go around to every; spiritualist, psychics, and anyone who deals with the occult and find him. I know he will have a link to one of these. That is the only way our killer has found out about these cult members and able to move in and out of these circles is to be part of it somehow. So today let's go to as many psychic shops as we can maybe we'll catch a break."

"Sounds good to me."

"But first let's finish up here and get back to the precinct to interview last night's victim. What's her name?"

"Emily Rosen," James answered looking at his notebook. "She's a student at OSU, she lives in campus housing, but they are bringing her in now. She should be at the precinct by the time we get there. Also I got word back on Kingston's background; it looks like he moved to Columbus eight years ago from Detroit Michigan. He had one prior for carry a concealed weapon, otherwise clean record."

"Okay let get out of here and head to the precinct," Sarah said. Her thoughts racing so fast they were nearly overwhelming. So many things to do, so many things happening at once it was nearly getting the best of her. She just hoped that she wouldn't fail.

James followed her out of the old house taking a breath of fresh air once they got outside and headed for her patrol car. He was hoping she wouldn't drive like a bat out of hell going back to the station.

"Let's go James," Sarah said as she got into her unmarked cruiser.

Thankfully she didn't drive too badly this time. By the time they got there Emily was already seated at Sarah's desk.

"Hi Ms. Rosen; my name is Detective Breckenridge and this is Detective Colburn. How are you doing?" Sarah asked.

"How do you think? I was kidnapped and nearly killed. Thank god I escaped."

"We are looking for the man who done this to you. We know who he is and have issued an ABP, hopefully we will find him," Sarah said trying to comfort her. Yet Emily didn't seem scared about him still being out there.

"All I want is to get some sleep, I'm worn out," Emily said yawning.

"Aren't you worried about the man who kidnapped you?"

"Not really, I figure he's on the run and won't bother me again."

"Do you know the man or seen him before?"

"No."

"How did you escape?"

"He went out and as soon as he did I was able to get out of my restraints and I ran out into the street screaming for help and a guy stopped."

"Is that how you called 911?"

"Yes he let me use his phone and then left right before the cops came."

"Why didn't the man wait until the police arrive?"

"I told you I don't know," Emily said her anger rising.

"Can you describe him?" Sarah ask, pushing for as much information as she could get.

"Yeah he was kind of tall, dark haired white guy. Look it was dark and I was scared and just glad to be alive."

"I understand Emily, but any information, even the smallest detail may be able to help us find him. He may have seen your kidnapper leaving the house."

"Like I said it was dark."

"Could you give us a minute please? While you wait would you like something to drink, water or coffee?" Colburn asked.

"Coffee with cream please."

"Coming right up."

"Detective Breckenridge would you help me a minute?" Colburn ask.

"Sure," Sarah said.

Once they walked over to where the coffee pot was. "What the hell are you doing James?"

"She's hiding the fact that someone helped her escape and she's not going to tell us shit if you keep badgering her. We have to gain her trust. Don't you see?"

"See what?"

"The person who helped her could be the Vendetta Killer. I've questioned a lot of witnesses, enough to know when someone is holding back. She'll clam up if you go at her hard. After all this man saved her life, there's no way she's going to give him up easily."

"James we don't have time, the press is going to have a field day now that there's a witness. When this hits the news we are going to have possible copycats out there trying to do the same thing and innocent people are going to die if we don't get a handle on this."

"I know, but please trust me on this one," James pleaded.

He fixed coffee for her and went back over to where Emily was sitting.

"Here ya go," James said gently.

"Emily, I'd like to put a police detail on you just in case this guy comes back after you. His name is Markius Demarkov and from the looks of it he is a serial killer, you're not safe," James said.

"I don't have anything to worry about," Emily slipped.

"What do you mean you don't have anything to worry about?" James ask picking up on her slip.

"Just that you guys found his house and I figure he's on the run and I'm the least of his worries."

"Emily, Demarkov is a serial killer and that place could be one of many he has. Once he has a target in mind he won't stop until he has you," James was pressing her trying to get more information about the anonymous man who helped her. He knew there was more to the story than what she was saying. There was no way she could have escaped on her own. He knew she had help and it must have been the Vendetta Killer.

"Do what you need to do detective I'm not going to live in fear. I have a life to live."

"I understand; we will have two plain clothes officers take you back to your dorm and watch you on campus, they won't be noticeable. Also please don't speak to the press."

"We will do all we can to keep your name out of the news. Here's my card in case you remember anything else or if you need me," Sarah told her leaving the fact that Demarkov was believed to be dead. Sarah knew Emily was holding back and not telling them everything. She couldn't blame her, whoever it was saved her life.

"One last thing, is this the man who kidnapped you," Sarah said showing her a photo of Demarkov.

"Yes," Emily shuttered.

"Would you mind to meet with our sketch artist and see if you can remember enough to give us a description of the man whose cell phone you used?" Sarah ask.

"No, like I told you I didn't get a good look at him."

"Could you talk with our FBI profiler then?"

"No, all I want to do is leave and get some rest," Emily said getting aggravated.

"Okay we'll have the officers drop you off at your dorm."

As soon as Emily left, Captain Harris called them into his office.

"Okay what do you have so far?" Harris ask.

"A pile of ashes was left at the thirteenth precinct with a letter and thumb. Same thing that happened here," Sarah answered.

"Okay I've called the Chief of Police and we are installing cameras at every precinct, it should be done by this evening."

"I think this guy is too smart to be caught on camera."

"You got a better idea?" Harris rebutted.

"Emily is the key to us finding the Vendetta Killer; apparently this man is not interested in hurting innocent people. Also he is not afraid to show his face, however it's going to be damn near impossible for us to get through to her. She is not going to hand him over to us. All we can do is wait and watch."

"In the meantime the press is on its way, the Chief has called a press conference to try and get a handle on it. We've already had two attacks on two men on Main Street. The attackers claimed they were about to attack a woman. One of the attackers is in the hospital with a broken jaw and four broken ribs. We can't let this get out of hand. It seems the entire city is on the Vendetta Killer's side. We are going to have vigilantes hurting or possible killing people if this keeps up," Captain Harris said.

"We understand sir," Sarah was the first to speak.

"You do; do you?" the Captain snapped back. "Even your dad the mayor is feeling the heat from this and after the press conference today it's only going to intensify."

"We've got a break in the case, we have a witness," Colburn interjected.

"Really? One who won't talk? Hell I don't blame her, who knows how many freaks are involved in this damn cult. Get a report together; I want it within the hour. Is that clear?" Harris said.

"Yes Captain," both Breckenridge and Colburn said at the same time and backed out of the office.

"Damn he's one tough son-of-a-bitch," Colburn said in a low voice.

"You heard him, let's get to work. Now that there's been a kidnapping that makes it a federal case and the FBI are sure to take over that case and hopefully they won't try to take over our case as well. I've asked that all the evidence be brought over and set up a command center so we can coordinate everything from here," Sarah told James.

"Who's going to be the liaison between us and the county and state police?"

"Sergeant Briggs for the state and Deputy Skaggs for the county police; the FBI has assigned Special Agent Adams as our go between with us. Me and you are lead investigators on this case. So get on the phone and find out if the evidence has arrived, also make sure they've taken a water sample from the water tank at Kingston's. And I want pictures from floor to ceiling, every square inch of that room."

"Got it," James said getting out his phone. After a minute, "yes thank you very much," James hung up. "The ashes and thumb are in the ME's office."

"Great let's go," Sarah said getting up.

"Right behind you."

They walked over to the ME's office. Dr. Daniels was in the middle of sorting everything.

"Hello detectives. I was wondering how long it would take you to get over here. I haven't had a chance to go through everything yet; however it looks just like the ones before. Everything's the same; of course I'm going to have to analyze the ashes. I've already ran the thumb print and it belongs to one Markius Kingston. The letter and envelope have been checked for prints and nothing was found."

"Just like the crime scene," James said.

"Captain Harris wants us both at the press conference. As soon as that's over I want to go back to Kingston's house and take a look around. We've got to get inside the mind of the Vendetta Killer if we are ever going to catch him," Sarah said.

"Okay."

"What's on your mind?"

"It's just this guy were after, we are never going to catch him. There's no way anyone is going to turn him in. Just like Emily Rosen, you know she saw his face and he may have even saved her from being killed by Kingston. Yet she wouldn't give us the time of day and was too certain about Kingston not coming after her. She knew he's dead, and that's why she wasn't worried. Also we tried to track the cell phone she used to call 911 and it was an unregistered prepaid phone that is not active now, which means it was ditched right after the call."

"You may be right James, but we are increasing patrols and we are going to use all available manpower until we catch him."

"Even if we catch him we don't have any fingerprints, no DNA, and no connection to the victims and most of all we don't have any bodies. There's no way the D.A. will take on a case with purely circumstantial evidence."

"We're going to have to catch him in the act. As far as we know we have three victims; Carlson, Demarkov, and now Kingston. The real question is: has he stopped killing? Because if he has we'll never find him, also they must be some connection between the three. If we can find it then it will tell us how many are in this cult. Because I believe the killings will stop when the Vendetta Killer runs out of members."

"True, but how are we going to deal with the press?"

"Leave that up to me after all, my dad is the mayor. I grew up with reporters following us everywhere."

"Is that why you're always on guard about your appearance and your conversations?"

"You're growing some big balls asking me questions like that," Sarah retorted.

"Sorry if I went too far, I didn't mean to make you feel uncomfortable. I was just trying to figure you out is all."

"Growing up the way I did everything you done was micro analyzed. It makes it hard to relate to people, you're always wondering if they are working some angle. I'm sorry if I come off rude or stand-offish," Sarah admitted.

"It's okay, I understand," James said. Actually he would forgive her of anything. He couldn't figure out why he was so attracted to her, but it was undeniable that he was falling hard for her. He hoped Sarah didn't notice.

"So now that's out of the way; let's get a preliminary report together before the Captain rips our ass."

"You got it."

All three murders had the exact same M.O. and so far we are focusing on one suspect, but no real motive, body, or murder weapon for that matter. The only real evidence was the letters; thumbs, and ashes. However now they had a witness that could possibly provide them with a positive identification of the killer and yet refused to due to the fact that he saved her life. And who could blame her. Her description of Kingston was spot on and yet all they had was ashes; a letter, and another damn thumb.

"James why do you think the Vendetta Killer is cutting the thumb off each of our victims?"

"Well it's a sure fire way to identify someone and without it a person cannot work his hand the same way like working things or grasping," James answered.

"I hadn't thought of it like that. I think he is cutting off both thumbs and keeping one and giving us the other so we can identify the victim. The profiler Agent Thomson said that our suspect is keeping trophies and that's why he may be keeping one thumb for himself."

"I agree, but how is this guy getting personal information on our victims?"

"He must have been part of them; it's the only thing that makes sense."

"Or he's a psychic," James said off-handed.

"Which reminds me, we got to get started running down the psychics who operate in the city."

"First we can run down anyone who has any priors."

"Get us a list together while I handle the press conference and give the Captain our report."

"Sure I hate dealing with either one," James said happily sliding into her seat.

"When I get back we will start running down the most promising leads after we go back to Kingston's house. I want one more look at things there and see if they have pulled any victims from the river. I'll have some uniforms check on those on the outskirts of town."

"Sounds like a plan," James said already busy writing down a priority list.

"Also please set up an end of day meeting with the FBI team. I want to compare notes again and see if they can refine the profile of our killer."

"Sure," James replied not taking his eyes off the computer screen, making a mental note of what she said. He wanted to refine the priority list more and focus on the most popular along with any who had a criminal background. Also any who has helped authorities in the past, although he didn't believe in such things he didn't want to be closed minded.

"Well that was brutal," Sarah said walking up to where James was seated still taking notes.

"Better you than me, I've hate dealing with them," James said smiling.

"Did you have a chance to set up a meeting with the FBI team this evening?"

"Yes, I called Agent Thompson and he will be here with two more teams they are bringing in. I set the meeting for five o'clock," James answered.

"Okay let's run back to Kingston's house and then start on the psychic list," Sarah said.

"Let's roll," James said eagerly. "I've also sent out a list of five each to four uniforms so they can get to running them down and I saved five priority ones for us to run down," James told her as they walked out of the precinct.

"So that's twenty-five total, that's not too bad."

"Just hope one of them pans out."

"Let's get to Kingston's place and then we can see if they do," Sarah said as they got into her cruiser. Damn James hated riding with others especially after he seen how she drove.

"Damn I can't believe how fast this case is moving, by this evening it will be national news."

"That's what worries me, we don't need people trying to copycat the Vendetta Killer and the longer this case goes the higher the chances of it happening," Sarah said grimly taking a corner too fast. "Sorry James, I know my driving scares you," she said slowing down.

"It's not the driving that scares me it's the wrecking I don't like," James said with a small laugh trying to appear brave.

"Don't worry I won't wreck you," Sarah said confidently, turning onto the street leading to the waterfront.

There was a flurry of activity happening, more than Colburn had ever seen on a crime scene.

"I'll go and see what CSU found; can you go and see what the dive teams found?" Sarah ask.

"Of course, divide and conquer," James replied walking in the direction of the river. Although it didn't take him long to know if they had been a murder due to the fact of three body bags lying on the ground. He walked up to one of the crime scene investigators and asked who was in charge.

"Tom Reynolds," he was told by nearby team member who pointed him out in the crowd. He was a tall middle aged man with graying hair standing by a transport van waiting to take the bodies to the medical examiners.

"Hello Mr. Reynolds I'm Detective Colburn," James introduced himself.

"Hello detective; quite the crime scene; I've never seen anything like it in the twenty years I've been doing this. So far the divers have pulled up three victims and there may be more. They just got another boat to help drag the opposite side of the river while divers focus on this side. I don't have a cause of death or time. You'll have to wait until we can get them to the morgue and do a full autopsy," Reynolds told James.

"Can you tell if it's foul play?" James ask.

"Each victim is a female early to mid-twenties, no noticeable cause of death, but each one had weights so they wouldn't float back up or be swept downstream by the rivers current. So as far as I can tell you can add three more murdered victims to your body count and possible more to come," Reynolds said.

"Anything else?" James ask.

"It's going to be hard to determine cause of death and how long they've been dead due to the fact of them being in the river. Also any trace evidence will have more than likely been washed away. I'll do my best, but don't count on having any answers until at lease a day or two and that's if we don't pull up anymore victims," Reynolds answered

"Here's my number if you find anything before I get back to you. I'll call you this evening and then touch base with you tomorrow morning."

"Sure thing," he said before turning back to the van to get the bodies loaded.

Everything was moving so fast he was worried that he wasn't going to be able to keep up. He always took pride in his work and it was just his luck that this case was blowing up bigger than anyone could have imagined. He knew there would be hell to pay if he screwed up in the least. All this was playing through his mind as he walked through the front door of Kingston's house. He knew where Sarah would be, right in the middle of everything. It came so natural to her he thought as he watched her going over the strange symbols in the walls down stairs in the sanctum.

"James," she called out to him.

"I can't believe how weird this case is," James said walking up to her.

"So what's the story outside?"

"They've pulled three female victims from the river so far," James told her and filled her in on the rest of the information or the lack thereof, which annoyed her immensely.

"They have only found two sets of prints down here. I having them ran now, but I'd bet they will be from Kingston and the victim. May be we'll catch a break and the Vendetta Killer slipped up this time leaving a set of prints behind."

"Anything else?"

"Unfortunately the place is clean otherwise. I'm having the water tested for any traces of DNA, but it's not looking promising."

"Don't worry we have the; FBI, city, county, and the state police on the hunt. It's just a matter of time before we catch him," James said trying to do his best to remain positive.

She knew James was trying to make her feel better about the case. Yet in reality she knew they were screwed.

"Thanks James I appreciate your positive attitude."

"Have you been able to determine if Kingston's house is linked in any way to Carlson's and Demarkov's?"

"To some extent all three are using some of the same symbols except changing the elemental symbols. Carlson's was Earth; Demarkov's was Fire, and Kingston's was water," she told James as she pointed to the center of the wall. "Here is the water element sign. See how it is centered and larger than the rest of the symbols which are in a circle around it."

"I see," James answered before asking, "Where's the altar?"

"I see you've been paying attention. It's over here; it was hidden underneath the water tank," she told him walking over to it. She pushed down on a small brick in the floor and the altar slid slowly and silently out to the front of the tank.

"Now you can see it has the same voodoo elements in it as the other two had."

"You're right," James said as he knelt down to get a closer look and take a couple of pictures to study later. Then something shiny caught his eye on the right side. He stood up and walked over to where he saw the object. It was a cluster of clear tubes and stainless steel plumbing fixtures. "What's this?"

"I think it's a way to refill the tank and over here on the left is a way to drain it. From what I can tell James is that each killer was trying to distill an essence from their victims. I'm convinced now more than ever that my hunch has been right all along."

"About what?"

"That each killer is taking the essence of the victims in the manner of the element they worshipped. Carlson buried his victims alive; Demarkov burned his victims to death, and now Kingston drowns his. That explains their use of alchemy and voodoo symbols. They are trying to make the Elixir of Life to extent their life forever," Sarah said breathlessly.

"No way, I don't believe it," James said stunned.

"It doesn't matter if we believe it or not, it's what our killers believed and the reason behind their actions. We now know their motive and can figure out whose left."

"Well according to the elements we have air and spirit left."

"And going by the ranking of the elements, the air killer will be the next to die and then spirit. If we don't catch the Vendetta Killer by then we may never get him." Sarah paused. "Okay we got to get running down that list of psychics. That is going to be the best chance we have of getting into the circle they run in. I know one who is the best in the city, Madam Marlena," Sarah finished.

"You're right; how did you know? She is at the top of my list."

"You forget I study this," Sarah said refreshing his memory about her field of studies in college. "Although psychics and gypsies aren't a well-defined religious group I still keep up on them."

"Is this Madam Marlena the real deal?"

"She's good, she actually helped me on a case when I first started in homicide. She has incredible perception skills, but there's more to her than that."

"You're not telling me you believe in all this; are you?"

"All I know is that there are things we can't understand."

Chapter 16 Blessings

"First I need to run to a cellular store to get another phone," Sam told Alana.

"I'm right here beside you," Alana smiled.

Sam knew a little about technology even though he rarely used it. He could use a computer and cell phones. Jacquelyn always wanted him to keep a cell phone even if it was just a simple flip phone for emergencies. Otherwise he preferred not to have anything at all, but he would do it to keep her happy.

After stopping by the nearest cell store he headed for Marlena's, which didn't take long. He pulled into her driveway and parked the truck and got out and walked to the front door which swung open before he could knock.

"How are you my dear Sam? So good to see you," Marlena said with a wide smile.

"I'm doing good, how are you?"

"I'm good. Come in, come in my dear," Marlena said opening the door wide.

"Oh Sam it's always so good to see you. I miss your visits so much. Please come in and make yourself at home while I make you a fresh cup of coffee," Marlena said beckoning him to the living room before disappearing into the kitchen. After a minute she walked back into the living room with a steaming hot cup of black coffee.

"Here you go dear," Marlena said putting it down on the coffee table in front of the old couch. "I see your mission is going well."

"It is; Carlson, Demarkov, and Kingston are dead. We have two left in this Avox group," Sam confirmed.

"So now you have Victor Vorgol and Logar Grunin, but Sam my dear boy you must be careful and your planning must be exact or you will not secede," Marlena said firmly.

"With you and Alana's help, how can I fail?" Sam said smiling.

"The blessings I do will last only twenty-four hours. So you must be careful and act before they run out. If they do you will be at the mercy of Vorgol's traps."

"I will and Alana will be with me."

"Always my love. Although I have grown in strength my power is not enough to defeat Vorgol, not without Marlena's help," Alana spoke up.

"So what do we need to do for the blessings?" Sam ask.

"I have everything ready, don't worry," Marlena said getting up to get Sam's empty coffee cup to get him a refill. "I'll be right back."

She came back into the living room carrying a small silver tray with coffee and sugar spiced cookies, his favorite.

"You know me well," Sam stood to take the tray from her and sat it down on the coffee table in front of the couch.

"Thank you," Sam said already taking a sip of the coffee. "Mmm my favorite," he told her.

"I don't forget what you like. Now about the blessings; once you're in Vorgol's lair and the wards are activated they will destroy the blessings I bestow upon you, but you will be unharmed. After that you must get to Vorgol before he can reset the wards."

"What about Alana? Will she be in any danger?"

"Yes she will Sam; Vorgol is master of the Air Element and has some power in the spirit realm.

However my blessings should be enough to protect her and long as you deal with Vorgol quickly. Remember he is more powerful than the others you've faced. You must not underestimate him, if you do he will kill you."

"God I hope he tries," Sam said with a wild look in his eyes. He could switch emotions in a split second when he was off his medicine. He enjoyed feeling so alive and pushing it to the brink of death. The adrenaline rush sent him into pure ecstasy.

"Sam be careful what you wish for," Alana warned.

"How do these blessings work?" Sam asked Marlena cutting Alana off from saying anything else.

"Well I have prepared special holy oil to anoint you with," Marlena said.

"What about Alana?" Sam ask

"While I can't physically anoint her I will bless her and place an ancient counter ward upon her so she will not be harmed. However once you're in his sanctum do your best to avoid any in there."

"How can we tell where they are?"

"They will be a special symbol carved into the walls or floor. Alana will be able to cause them to glow."

Sam finished his coffee, "Let's get to it then," he said smiling.

"You were never one to waste time," Marlena said getting to her feet. "Follow me dear," she said walking through the door leading to the kitchen. She opened another door that lead downstairs into the basement.

"Down here," she said turning on the stairwell light and started down the steps. Sam followed her obediently with Alana behind him.

"This is my worship room Sam," Marlena said as she turned on the light revealing a room that was filled with golden statues, signs and symbols from floor to ceiling with an altar at the far end.

"Wow, I've never seen anything like it," Sam said in amazement.

"You have, but you don't remember," Marlena said as they walked up to the altar. "Now I want you and Alana to stand in front of the altar," she instructed as she walked around and stood behind. She put on a purple robe emblazoned with gold symbols and then she put on a gold tiara making her look like a priestess Sam thought.

"Sam my dear would you please kneel before the altar?" Marlena ask.

'Of course," Sam complied.

"Alana," Marlena looked over at her and she knelt in her ghostly form.

"Will you accept the blessings I am about to bestow?"

"Yes."

"Sam will you accept the blessings I am about to bestow?"

"Yes."

Marlena's voice began to change, echoing in the room. She was speaking in a language Sam couldn't understand. She spread her arms and brought them together with open hands. Sam felt a force come from them that nearly knocked him backwards. He felt a tingling from the top of his head to the bottom of his feet. Alana's form shimmered with a golden light. Marlena spread her arms again speaking words he could not understand. She brought them together again. Another more powerful force hit him, this time he was prepared, but it still nearly caused him to fall backwards. He felt an incredible amount of strength pulsate though his body. This time it blinded him with pure white light. He looked over at Alana as her form glistened.

"Sam don't fight it," Marlena told him, sensing he was.

"I'm trying."

"Everything will be okay and you will be protected if you fully accept my blessings."

"I accept your blessings," Sam said relaxing his body and mind.

"Now Sam; Alana I need you to clear your minds of any thoughts," Marlena told them. Her voice grew more powerful and forceful as she spoke to place the last blessing on them.

Sam's mind seemed to be traveling out of darkness to a place of bathed blinding golden light. He felt his body tremble with power as he accepted the blessing. Then he opened his eyes and saw everything was glowing with a golden light even her and Alana was bathed in it. He felt so incredibly powerful like nothing could hurt him, even his mind was more focused than ever with a sole thought of killing Vorgol. Chills ran though his body causing him to shake; finally the light faded and everything came into focus.

Marlena looked pale and as she was about to faint. Sam stood up and walked around the altar to give her a hand.

"Are you okay?"

"I will be, it takes a lot out of me when I do these. I haven't done them in a very long time."

"I'm sorry," Sam said holding her hand.

"Here please take my robe and tiara and place them in the box here," Marlena said taking them off.

Sam did as she asked and then held Marlena's arm as she walked around the altar.

"Let's go upstairs and I'll get you something to drink."

"Thank you," she said in a weakened voice.

"Alana is there anything you can do to help

her regain her strength?"

"Here Marlena," she touched her shoulder her form shimmered a little. Marlena's color returned.

"Much better my dear; thank you Alana," Marlena's voice sounded much stronger.

"Now let's get you upstairs," Sam said still holding her arm.

They went upstairs and Marlena sat in her chair and took a deep breath.

"My dear Sam," Marlena said.
"What is it?" Sam asked gently.

"I've seen a vision of two people who may get in your way. You must avoid them at all cost. If you don't you won't be able to finish your mission."

"Who are they?"

"I saw a man and a woman investigating the others and may prevent you from killing Vorgol and Grunin. They are detectives with the Columbus police."

"I will be careful, don't worry."

"Sam they're here," Marlena said suddenly.

"What do you want me to do?"

"Go into the kitchen while I meet with them in the parlor. Do not harm them they are only doing their job."

"I'll do as you ask."

"They're at the front door, I must go."

"But you're weak," Sam protested.

"I have strength enough for this. Now go to the kitchen please Sam; I'm okay," Marlena said getting to her feet.

"Okay, but if you need me I'm here," Sam told her and walked to the kitchen.

"I hate this," Sam said.

"What?" Alana ask.

"I feel the need to protect her."

"They are just cops doing their job."

"Can you go and see what they want?"

"As you wish darling," Alana said and vanished from sight.

Sam hated the thought of Marlena getting into trouble with the law over helping him. He would stand responsible for what he done, however he knew deep down he wasn't going to stop. One he started something he would finish it even if it killed him in the end.

Sam inched his way to the doorway trying to overhear their conversation, however he could only pick up a few words here and there. He couldn't risk getting any closer to the front parlor. He heard shuffling of feet and the front door open and close. He stepped back into the kitchen and waited on Marlena to return.

"It's clear Sam they're gone," Marlena called out from the living room.

Sam walked back into the living room; Marlena was already seated in her chair.

"How much do they know?" Sam ask as he sat down on the couch.

"It was Detective Breckenridge and Detective Colburn. I had helped Detective Breckenridge in the past on a missing person's case. We have to be extremely careful going forward."

"What did she ask you?"

"She has figured that the three you killed are in a cult, but she doesn't know about the Avox though. However she's knows Victor Vorgol, that he's a professor at OSU and she has seen him about this case."

"I see," Sam said already thinking about Vorgol. "After tonight he will not be able to help anyone."

"After tonight she will redouble her efforts to find you. You must be at your best when you take him out."

"I am at my best since I've stopped taking my medications, although my memories haven't come back yet," Sam said.

"They will, be patient. You have come to a point where you can handle them and I can help, but we must go slowly. I'll show you," Marlena said getting out of her chair and walked over and stood in front of him. "Be still and clear your mind," she told him.

"Okay," Sam obeyed without question.

Marlena placed her aged hands on top of Sam's head; he remained still. He could see scenes of David his best friend and then they changed to his sister. She was so young and beautiful; he breathed deeply trying to take in every detail, how much he loved her. The pain was unbearable, he snapped out of it as soon as Marlena took her hands away.

"Are you okay dear? I'm sorry if that was too much to deal with at one time."

"No it's okay; it gives me strength to carry on."

"Let me get you a cup of coffee," Marlena said turning to go into the kitchen. She came back with a steaming hot cup.

"Thank you."

"You're welcome dear."

Sam took a sip and sat the coffee down. "What should I do about the cops?"

"Sam do not hurt them, they are only doing their job."

"I'll do my best, but I cannot have anyone get in the way. I will try not to kill them," Sam said through clenched teeth.

"Sam my love you cannot kill innocents," this time it was Alana speaking. "We will be able to avoid them I will ensure it," she promised.

"You're right I'm sorry I ever considered it. I worry about being able to stay in control of my emotions…," Sam trailed off.

Alana cut in, "darling we are here for you, with our help you shall overcome anything."

"Thank you both for all your help. I couldn't make it without you," Sam told them with a smile.

"Anything for you my dear Sam," Marlena said tearing up.

"I will always be at your side," Alana said.

This comforted him greatly. "With you two on my side how can I fail?" Sam's mind jolted a second with images of his best friend.

"You okay Sam?" Marlena ask.

"Yes, I just had a memory of David; he loved you very much," Sam said in a warm rich tone.

"Thank you my dear Sam, thank you so much," Marlena said getting to her feet and walked over and gave Sam a hug. "David thought the world of you Sam."

"I know," Sam choked back tears; his emotions screamed throughout his body trembled. Marlena hugged him tighter and he finally relaxed.

"Thank you Marlena."

"Now let's go over our plan," Alana spoke up changing the subject.

Marlena sat back down in her chair and Sam sat back down on the old couch.

"Vorgol should be in his home tonight, once we're there I will go in first to activate the wards," Alana said.

"No," Sam cut in. "You'll get hurt."

"You will need your blessings intact for the inner sanctum. I will not be hurt. He is powerful, but I have grown in strength and will be okay."

"Are you sure?"

"My love I would never lie to you," Alana told him.

"I know; okay then it's settled you will go in first until we reach the inner sanctum and then I will go in. Once his traps are triggered and out of our way you will come in and help subdue Vorgol."

"It's a good plan," Marlena said.

"I agree," Alana said.

"Okay with me," Sam confirmed.

"Let me get you another cup of coffee Sam," Marlena said making her way to the kitchen. She returned with a steaming hot cup of coffee. "Here you go dear; are you hungry?"

"No I'm good," Sam said smiling. Some days

he wouldn't eat just drink coffee all day; it never made him nervous or jittery.

"You were never one to eat much."

"You know me so well," Sam smiled.

"Eat my love, you'll need your strength tonight," Alana told him.

"I'll eat when I get home," Sam offered a compromise.

"Make sure you do," Marlena said in a motherly tone.

"I will, I promise," Sam smiled, then thought of having not one but three women nagging at him made him laugh.

"What's so funny?" Marlena ask.

"It's just I have three women making sure I take care of myself."

"You need it, you're hard headed," Alana said.

"I agree," Marlena chimed in smiling.

"Oh look at the time," Sam said looking at his wristwatch. "I got to go. Thank you for your blessings Marlena," Sam said standing up.

Marlena got to her feet and walked over to Sam and gave him a hug. "Thank you for spending time with me. You mean the world to me, please be careful tonight when you deal with Vorgol."

"I will, don't worry," Sam said hugging her

tightly. Marlena was in tears again.

"What's wrong?"

"I can't bear the thought of anything happening to you," Marlena wept.

"Shh its okay, everything will be okay, after all I have your blessings and Alana will be right by my side," Sam reassured her. He felt her relax her hug.

"I'm sorry for getting emotional," Marlena looked up at him with tear stained eyes. Sam placed his right hand on her cheek, "I promise everything will be okay, destiny is on our side," he assured her again.

"It is," she smiled.

"I will send Alana to you as soon as it's over," Sam offered.

"Thank you," Marlena said getting a white handkerchief from her dress pocket and wiped her face.

"We better get going Alana," Sam said.

"I'm ready," Alana said.

Sam gave Marlena another quick hug and walked out and got into his truck.

"Damn," Sam said angrily.

"What is it my love?"

'The cops that were here may have written

down my license plate number."

"I will find them and see."

"Would you?"

"Of course my love anything for you; I will meet you back at your house. It will take me a little time to locate them."

"Thanks so much," Sam said tenderly.

"You're very welcome darling," Alana's ghostly hand caressed his cheek.

Sam felt a cool touch on his right cheek. "I'll see you soon." Sam smiled as he started his truck and backed out. His mind on Vorgol he nearly hit a passing car. It was hard for him to multitask; he cleared his mind and focused on driving. He would have time to think once he got home. It didn't take him long to get home, traffic wasn't bad. He pulled into his driveway and parked his truck next to Jacquelyn's car got out and took a deep breath.

He wanted to spend some quantity time with Jacquelyn and the kids before his next kill. Although he couldn't shake and ominous feeling maybe he had let Marlena and Alana get to him and shake his confidence. He would have to psych himself up before taking on Vorgol. He knew he had to focus of his sister's murder and the memories he had just got from Marlena and not taking that damn medicine. The only thing that bothered him was the pleasure he received in killing the members of the Avox.

Although they were evil bastards and took

many lives; should he take pleasure in their deaths? He would have to sort that out later, he had a busy night to prepare for, he thought as he opened the front door and both kids came running.

"Daddy, daddy, you're home," Cassy said hugging him tightly along with Sammy vying for a spot. He reached down and picked Sammy up and hugged him and kissed him on his cheek.

"Daddy pick me up too," Cassy pleaded.

Sam knelt down and picked her up too and gave her a kiss.

"I love you daddy," Cassy said smiling.

"I love you both so much," Sam told them.

"And what do you think you're doing mister?" Jacquelyn ask with her arms crossed. "You know you have to be careful about lifting."

"I'm okay," Sam defended.

"Still you're not supposed to lift like that."

"Okay okay," Sam said kneeling down and let go of the kids.

"Now; how about a hug from mommy?" Sam smiled.

Jacquelyn could never resist him. He grabbed her and gave her a bear hug and lifted her off her feet kissing her.

"Boy what's gotten into you today?"

"Nothing, just had a great day at work and miss spending time with my beautiful wife and kids."

"Aww that's sweet babe, I love you," she said kissing him again.

"Now what's for dinner?"

Both kids laughed, "You missed dinner daddy," Cassy informed him.

"Oh no!" Sam said in an exaggerated tone.

"I saved you a plate babe. If you let me go I'll go and heat it up," Jacquelyn told him.

"One more kiss," Sam demanded.

"Okay," she kissed him again.

Sam let her go and followed into the kitchen. "I'm hungry. What did you fix?"

"Meatloaf."

"My favorite; I'll go wash up." It was one of the abilities since the accident was switching emotional states in a split second, especially when he wasn't taking his medicine. He washed up and headed back to the kitchen. Jacquelyn was a great cook, Sam never had any complaints.

"Thank you babe," Sam said sitting down at the dining room table.

"You're welcome, here you go," she said smiling sitting a plate piled high with mashed potatoes; gravy, green beans, and meatloaf.

"Ah looks so good," Sam said before digging in. He ate while Jacquelyn attended to the kids.

His thoughts turned to Vorgol, he would have to be at his best tonight to take him down, and Marlena's blessings would only go so far. Family right now he told himself. Sam finished eating and took his plate and glass over to the sink and rinsed them off just as Jacquelyn walked in.

"Was it good babe?"

"It was great baby, thanks so much," Sam gave her a kiss. "Now where are my little varmints?"

'They're playing in the living room, just waiting until bath time."

"I'll help you, you bathe Cassy and I'll bathe Sammy."

"Sound's great," Jacquelyn said as they walked into the living. Cassy was working a puzzle and Sammy was playing with his toy truck. Sam sat down between them; they always enjoyed it when he would play with them.

"Okay Cassy, it's time for your bath," Jacquelyn told her.

"Oh mommy, I haven't finished my puzzle," Cassy moped.

"You can work on it tomorrow; I'll leave it out for you, okay."

"Okay mommy," Cassy said standing up and

walked over to her.

"Would you like a bubble bath?"

Sam sat and played with Sammy until Jacquelyn came and got them. Sam bathed Sammy and dressed him in his favorite pajamas and put him in bed while Jacquelyn tended to Cassie. Sam tucked him in and kissed his forehead just as Jacquelyn came in.

"And where's my nighttime kiss?"

"Here mommy," Sammy said as Sam went to give Cassy a kiss goodnight.

"Daddy loves you honey," Sam told Cassy as he kissed her forehead. "Sweet dreams," he said as he left the room and closed the door just as Jacquelyn was closing Sammy's.

"Baby I'm going to take a shower; I won't be long," she told him.

"Okay I'll get one after you," Sam said as he walked to the living room. He had a thought and went to undress in the bedroom and quietly slipped into the master bathroom. He gently slid the shower curtain open, "You scared me," Jacquelyn said and then saw he was naked. "Oh I see now," she grinned as Sam climbed into the shower with her. He massaged her shoulders and neck, "oh god that feels so good baby," she moaned. This turned Sam on so much, he slid his strong hands around to play with her breast, fondling her nipples, she moaned louder. He kissed her neck and then she turned to him kissing him passionately wrapping her arms around his neck and her legs around his waist taking in everything he offered. The hot water streaming down her back intensified the in incredible feelings, "oh Sam," she moaned, "oh god you feel so good baby" she whispered in his ear. Which made him drive harder and faster; he could feel the climax coming. She tensed as he did as they both came together; she dug her nails into his back.

"Oh god baby that was phenomenal; I don't know what's gotten into you, but I like it," Jacquelyn said smiling and then kissed him.

"All you baby, all you; I love you," he said looking deep into her eyes.

"I love you to baby," she said looking up at him. God she loved him so much she thought as they finished showering. "It's been a long time since we done that, we should do that more often."

"Definitely."

They both got dressed in their pajamas and went to the kitchen. Sam wanted coffee and Jacquelyn wanted ice cream. After they got what they wanted they went into the living room and sat on the couch.

"I have to be in Cleveland in the morning first thing, I'll have to leave here around three a.m. to get there by five a.m. The men will be there at six a.m. and I want a chance to go over the plans and survey the area before they get there."

"You won't get much sleep babe; can't you leave later?"

"I could, but you know me," Sam said taking a drink of coffee.

"I know, but you know how much I worry about you," Jacquelyn said between bites of ice cream.

"Don't worry, I've got that cell phone in the truck, I'll call you as soon as I get there, okay."

"Please, that way I won't worry all day. Do you have that phone charged up and ready for use?"

"Yes baby, I always do; actually I just checked it today," he smiled thinking about the new one he had just bought earlier.

"Okay just be careful, if you get sleepy pull over and rest, you know your medicine makes you drowsy."

"I always do," Sam said and reached over and gave her a kiss. "Oh sweet lips," he smiled tasting the ice cream on her lips.

"Careful baby or they'll be a round two," warned Jacquelyn.

"Now you're talking," Sam said putting his coffee down and reached over and took her ice cream bowl and sat it on the coffee table. He stood up and walked over in front of her and scooped her up in his arms. God he loved the energy he had when he was off his medications.

"Baby…" she began to protest.

"Shh I'm fine honey," he said as he carried her to their bedroom giving her passionate kisses.

He nearly ripped her clothes off when he laid her down on the bed as she was undressing him. At first he was on top of her driving as deep as he could. He lifted up her legs to get into her even deeper. He rolled over and let her get on top to ride him, it was her favorite position, and she loved it when she was in full control. He moaned so loud loving every minute of it, as he held her hips, god she felt so amazing. She started going faster and faster, he couldn't wait until she exploded in wetness all over his rock hard cock. Finally he could feel her release and he let go grabbing her close to him their bare naked bodies together with nothing between them. She lay on top of him panting.

"Oh god that was incredible baby," she said through labored breaths.

"Phenomenal," Sam said drawing a deep breath hugging her tightly and kissed her. She rolled off him and cuddled next to him rubbing chest laying her head on his arm.

"I love you."

"I love you too baby," Sam said pulling her closer. He loved lying naked together, the feeling of her soft skin next to his. They laid there in happy bliss without a care in the world for a while.

"I'm going to get a quick shower," Jacquelyn

said and kissed him before getting out of bed.
God these moments were so wonderful he thought as
he got to his feet and went to the guest bathroom to
wash up and dress again; after which he went back
into the living room. He picked up his cup of now
cold coffee and Jacquelyn's bowl and went into the
kitchen and rinsed out the bowl and got him a fresh
cup of hot coffee and then returned to the living
room and sat down and waited for her to return.

"There you are," she said as she walked into
the living room.

"Just made myself a fresh cup of coffee," Sam
said as she sat beside him rubbing his neck and
shoulders.

"Have you taken your evening meds yet?"

"I did just now while I was in the kitchen."

"Baby I know you don't like to take your
medicine, but please for me and the kids take it, you
know it helps you so much."

"I know babe, don't worry I'm takings all my
meds," Sam lied.

"Good," she kissed him. "I'm going to take my
night meds, are you coming to bed?"

"I will shortly I have to go over some plans for
work and then I'll come to bed."

"Goodnight sweetheart," Jacquelyn said and
went to the kitchen to take her night medicine and
went to bed.

Chapter 17 The Avox

"Who do you have next on your list?" Sarah ask, turning the subject back to the list James made.

"Madam Andrea Malone, she's had a couple of priors ten years ago for fraud and theft by deception," James read from his notes.

"Okay, what's her address?"

"1021 Tenth Street over on the east side."

"Got it," Sarah said punching the address into her GPS unit.

"We'll try to interview one more after her and then head to headquarters to wrap things up. We have had a busy day; also the FBI forensics team is coming in to go over what they found at all the crime scenes. They may have found something that our teams missed during the first sweeps of the places."

"At this point we can use all the help we can get."

"We are still the lead investigators and maintain jurisdiction since all the murders have taken place in our city. That may change however if they connect any murders to our suspect which have taken place outside the state, then it would become a federal case. Let's hope it doesn't go that far," Sarah said as she pulled into Madam Andrea's driveway.

"Let's see what she can tell us," James said getting out of the car first.

"Hopefully more than the last one did; although I still feel she was withholding information from us," Sarah told James as they walked up the old sidewalk leading to the front door. It was a nondescript house like you would find anywhere with the exception of a small neon open sign in the front window beside the door. James knocked; it didn't take her long to answer indicating she wasn't with a client.

"Hello come in," said a middle aged woman who looked like she took pride in appearance; long black hair, glasses, slender build and not bad looking either James noticed. They followed her into the parlor where there was a small round table with a crystal ball in the center and white candles on each side, which she lit as she sat down.

"Please detectives sit; how can I be of

service?" Madam Andrea ask.

"How did you know we were detectives?" James ask.

"I keep up on the news; I knew it would be a matter of time before you guys would start interviewing every psychic in the city."

"So, do you know of any groups who would be responsible for these murders?" Sarah ask.

"Right to the point huh. From what I hear whoever killed the three mass murders are doing the city a favor."

"We cannot allow a vigilante to continue to do this." Sarah's temper began to rise. "If we don't stop him now things are going to get worse and before you know it we are going to have copycat killers out there and innocent people are going to get killed," Sarah warned.

"I may be able to help, but what's in it for me?"

"For one thing we can make sure that you never work in this city again. How do you think your clients would feel if they knew your past? Let's see there the theft by deception, oh and fraud, my what a colorful past you have."

"You wouldn't!" Andrea scowled.

"Oh yes we would," Sarah said frankly.

"The only way I will help you is if you keep

my name out of the investigation; will you?"

"Why?" James ask.

"Because I value my life and if you value yours you would drop the case and leave it alone," Andrea said with a frightened look.

"Let's us worry about our safety; as far as you go we will not mention you or put your name in any report. Do we have a deal?" Sarah ask.

"Okay here's what I know. A few years ago I had a run in with Carlson, he tried to get me to join this group called the Avox; each group consist of five people who use voodoo and alchemy in a bid for everlasting life. However I did not know they killed people until the news story broke, and then I put two and two together. I'm just so glad that I didn't join."

"So an Avox group consists of five people. Are they usually all male?" Sarah ask taking notes.

"Most are all men, that's why I was surprised when Carlson asked me to join."

"How many Avox groups are operating in the city?"

"I'm not sure, it was a long time ago."

"Please think hard, we need all the information we can get; anything will help."

"He talked about other groups operating in the city, but I think this was one of the first in the city. However I'm certain since then they have been more that's started."

"Do you know who would want to kill them?" this time it was James speaking.

"None that I know of, though from what I've been hearing it has to be someone who knows their inner workings, it's the only thing that makes sense."

"Did Carlson tell you about the other members?" James asked.

"No, like I said, I didn't join and I'm glad I didn't. Needless to say I wouldn't have lasted long once I found out that they were killing innocent women in their insane bid for immortally."

"Do you know any other psychics who know about the Avox?" Sarah jumped in.

"Only one I can think of is Madam Marlena. She's been in the business longer than I have."

"Why do you think she may know something?"

"I figured if they tried to recruit me it's only logical they would try to get her. I know she is very powerful and if anyone could do the things they wanted she could."

"Is there anything else you can tell us?"

"No like I said I never joined and after I turned them down I never heard from them again."

"Thank you so much for your cooperation; here's my card if you remember anything," Sarah said reaching her card and stood up. James followed her to the door and out to the car.

"You think she's telling us the truth?" James ask Sarah.

"I do, I just wonder why Marlena didn't tell us about the Avox, surely she would have known."

"Maybe she's afraid of them," James offered.

"Yeah, but maybe she's hiding her involvement. She could be setting up the victims for the Avox. This day and age we can not take anything for granted," Sarah reminded him.

"True," James agreed.

"We'll pay her a visit again first thing in the morning; right now we have to get back to the precinct to prepare for the morning conference and see if we have any tips that came in today."

"Don't you think we need to go to Marlena's first?"

"Right now I don't have anything, we have to dig into her life before we see her again; otherwise she is going to tell us the same thing. We have to find something that will get her to tell us everything or it will be a waste of time."

"When we get back to the station I will go through her life with a fine tooth comb. I've already checked for any priors and she doesn't have any. She had one child a son named David who was killed a little over ten years ago in a crane accident."

"Run a check on him and see if he was mixed up in any criminal activity that may link him to the Avox."

"He's been dead so long; how will that help us?"

"I know it's a long shot, but it's all we got to go on. Maybe it will lead us to someone else who' involved."

"You're right," James conceded.

It was dark by the time they got back to the station. James grabbed his files out of the car and him and Sarah walked into the department which was busier than usual. Everyone was putting in overtime trying to stay on top of the case. CSU was stretched thin doing their best to handle multiple crime scenes with the body count now standing at eleven and growing.

James and Sarah walked over to their white boards to regain their perspective of the case thus far.

"Okay so far we have three serial killers who were murdered by our unidentified subject," Sarah began.

"Whoever it is has to have intimate knowledge of them and we now know that Madam Andrea and possibly Marlena knew of Carlson, maybe more," James said writing their names on the board. "Andrea has no children and Marlena had one son who was killed in a construction accident. Maybe that's why Marlena joined the Avox," Sarah pondered.

"If she did that, it would be a good reason."

"And she may know our next target."

"How are we supposed to get a search warrant based on that?"

"We can't, but we can put her under surveillance."

"Worth a try," James said nodding his head.

"It's all we got and while we're at it I'll assign two plain clothes deputies to watch Andrea just in case she was trying to throw us off her trail."

"Good idea."

"If you're up for it we will go by Marlena's early in the morning before the briefing."

"What are you hoping to find?"

"Anything that can link her or her son to the Avox, something is bothering me about her, call it a gut feeling, but she knows far more than she is telling us."

"I'm with you," James said noticing the time. He had been building up the courage to ask Sarah out for a drink.

"Would you like to get a drink?" he ask nervously.

After a brief pause, "sure I can use one; this case is driving me nuts. James, I said yes, let's get out of here," she told a stunned James.

"Of course," James stammered.

"Where would you like to go?" she ask.

"I know a great little place close to here that has the best selection of craft beer in the city."

"Let's go," Sarah said grabbing her jacket and purse.

"I'll drive," James said as they walked out of the precinct, he had had enough of her driving for the day. It was hard to hide his nervousness; he felt that she was out of his league. He could be around her working and never felt as nervous as he did asking her out for a simple drink after a long day. He picked a nice but small pub called the Vue.

"This place has great food in case you're hungry," James said as he pulled into the parking lot and parked.

"A little, but right now I could go for a glass of wine," Sarah told him getting out of the car. He had gone around to open it for her, but she was half way out by the time he got there. "I've never been here."

"You'll enjoy it," James said confidently as they walked to the entrance, thankfully the place wasn't too busy being a weeknight. James picked out a booth in the far corner so they could have privacy. Within minutes a cute young waitress came over to take their order.

"I'll take a glass of merlot please," Sarah

ordered.

"I'll have a light beer please," James said.

"So what do you do in your spare time?" Sarah ask.

"Oh you know, travel the world in my private jet," James smiled causing Sarah to laugh.

"No seriously."

"You'll think it's silly."

"No, come on tell me," Sarah coaxed.

"Promise not to laugh?"

"Promise," Sarah said placing her right hand over her heart smiling.

"I like to listen to loud rock music while I paint," James replied waiting for her to laugh, but she just smiled. "Okay out with it."

"Well I must say I've never met a fellow cop who paints."

"I find that it takes away the stress of the day; so what do you do in your off time?" James ask, as the waitress brought them another round. Sarah took a drink before answering.

"Well when I get time, which is rare these days; I love to curl up to a good book and a large glass of wine. I know that's not exciting or daring, but the job provides plenty of that."

"I agree there, by the way are you hungry?"

"Sure what do you recommend?"

"They have the best Philly cheese steak in the city, we can spilt one of you want, they are pretty big."

"Sounds great."

James got the waitress' attention and she took their order. "Your food will be ready in a few minutes," she said politely and left.

Their conversation flowed so well like they had known each other for years. James finally relaxed enough to be himself and saw there was definitely a connection between them. Their conversation never skipped a beat even when the food was served. They could barely take a bite without laughing or talking. Time flew by and before they knew it, it was midnight.

"Would you like a nightcap at my place?" Sarah ask.

"Sure," James answered trying to sound cool and calm while the butterflies returned and adrenaline shot through him like a bolt of lightning.

"Here I'll get the check," James said and went to the bar to pay the tab.

"We're ready," James said as he reached the booth. They left the pub and drove to her apartment which wasn't far just over on the west side. It was a beautiful gated community.

"Nice," James said as he pulled up to the gate.

"It's okay for now, I don't have time to keep up a house," Sarah told him.

"Um, what's the gate code?" James ask.

"Four one three."

"Got it."

"Up there take a left, then right."

"No problem," James said as he parked the car.

They held hands as they walked up to her apartment. At the door she turned to him and shoved him up against the wall and kissed him with such passion that caught him completely off guard. "Wow," James murmured as she released her grip and unlocked her door. She turned the lights on and threw her keys into a glass dish on the sofa table. She started taking off her shirt as she walked towards her bedroom.

"You coming?" Sarah ask smiling.

"Oh yeah!" James answered unbuttoning his shirt. As he got to her she took a step forward and grabbed his waist and kissed him with such fervor it sent him into a frenzy taking off his shirt and unzipping his pants. By the time they reached the bedroom they were both naked. He was on top of her kissing her sweet tender nipples, licking them in circles. Taking his tongue and running down her beautiful stomach, making him even more aroused. Slowly he moved down to her inner thighs and then back up to her pussy. This sent her into an erotic ecstasy; she arched her back and moved her legs wider apart allowing him full access. He drove his tongue deeper into her soaking wet pussy. God he couldn't wait to plunge his rock hard cock into it, but he waited until he made her cum first. She groaned so loud he knew she was cumming. He smiled and then slid himself into her slowly at first, pushing her legs wider so he could penetrate her as deeply as he could, she groaned, "that's it baby, fuck me harder."

He pumped his cock harder and faster, "oh god you're amazing," he whispered into her ear as he kissed it and then ran his teeth down her neck teasing her with little love bites. Her heavy breathing turned him on even more. He was going to explode, faster, harder, deeper until they both came at the same time. For a minute they just laid there panting, skin on skin enveloped in ecstasy.

"Wow," James panted.

"God you were incredible," Sarah said and then kissed him.

"You were absolutely amazing," James told her rolling over to the side lying close to her and she turned to face him taking her hand and caressed his face. He gave her a kiss as they laid there looking into each other's eyes for what seemed an eternity.

"Join me for a shower?" Sarah ask.

"Sure," James smiled getting out of bed and followed her to the bathroom. The shower felt so good, even better sharing it with her. They made love again which felt great with the hot water running down their bare naked bodies. Each other feeling the other, they couldn't keep their hands off each other. Both were exhausted by the time they dried off and got back to the bed.

"Why don't you stay here tonight since we have to go to Marlena's first thing in the morning, it's already two am," Sarah told him.

"Sounds great as long as you don't snore," James laughed.

"Same goes for you, because if you do you'll have to sleep on the couch," Sarah laughed.

"Don't worry I don't, but I haven't slept with anyone in a long time."

"Me either, my work doesn't allow me much personal time."

"I know the feeling," James agreed.

"James please don't breath a word of this to anyone, otherwise we won't be able to work together and my father will go berserk if he finds out," Sarah warned him.

"Don't worry about me; I don't want to get busted down to traffic cop or worse a meter maid," James smiled weakly.

"Let's get a couple hours of sleep, I'll set the alarm," Sarah said as she got in bed and covered up with James getting in beside her. He lay on his back and Sarah laid her head on his chest and they both fell asleep right away smiling.

<u>Chapter 18 Dr. Vorgol</u>

"Hello my darling," came a familiar whisper from Alana.

Sam jerked a little surprised by her.

"Hello Alana," Sam said still distracted by the thoughts of his love making sessions with Jacquelyn.

"Were you able to find those two detectives?" Sam ask snapping back to thinking about the day's events and the upcoming fight with Vorgol.

"Yes darling I was able to find them and they did not take down your license plate number."

"Good, we'll have to be more careful from now on."

"There are increased police presence in the city tonight due to the other kills."

"We'll be okay, we just need to be extra careful and not make any mistakes."

"I've also learned that Detective Breckenridge has had classes under Vorgol at the university. I don't know if she had any relationship with him outside of school," Alana said.

"Interesting; what about the other detective?"

"His name is Detective Colburn and he is an honorable man. They are questioning all the psychics in the city, though none of them know of Marlena's real power."

"That's good."

"Vorgol is in his home tonight, I checked before I came here."

"Good," Sam said still a little distracted.

"Sam my love please concentrate, you must be at your best when you fight Vorgol."

"I'm sorry Alana, you're right. Now how many has this bastard murdered?"

"Six my love, once he was done with them he buried them at an old industrial complex at the north end of the city."

"After tonight he will murder no more," Sam grinded his teeth thinking of the innocent lives that the no good son-of-a-bitch took.

"That's better," Alana coached him. "Think of your sister, we must succeed for her." She could feel the rage building in Sam like a slumbering volcano about to awaken. Sam trembled with the desire for vengeance, for justice for the innocent victims of the murderer he was going to face tonight.

"I have to prepare a special bag in case we need in."

"Yes my love," Alana smiled.

"I'll check on Jacquelyn and the kids first," Sam said getting to his feet still a little weakened from the evening's activities. "I'll be right back."

"I'll wait here my love."

Sam went into his bedroom first and gave Jacquelyn a light kiss of her forehead. "Love you," he whispered. Then he repeated it with the kids telling each of them he loved them. He knew he may not come back if he failed in his mission tonight.

"All done," he said in a low voice as he walked back into the living room.
"Sam I have one more blessing I would like to bestow upon you tonight before we leave."

"What it is?"

"One that will allow me to take any damage directed at you."

"No, I will not allow you to be harmed," Sam said angrily.

"My love I can heal quicker than you, there is only so much damage that I can heal you from," Alana pleaded.

"No Alana, don't worry Marlena's blessings

will be enough to see us through. And we have God Almighty on our side of this righteous battle. Marlena may have summoned you, but God sent you to aid me in this quest for justice. We will not fail, be confident, be strong in our hour of need," Sam urged her.

"Yes my love you're right, we shall win this battle and continue to carry our fight to our enemies," Alana spoke boldly with renewed energy.

"Yes we shall," Sam agreed and went to pack an over night bag. He was used to going out of town for a day or two.

"I'll need to stop at the superstore for a couple of items I might need if things get messy," Sam told Alana as he placed the remaining things into his bag and went into the kitchen to make fresh coffee and fill his thermos' and got his medicines so Jacquelyn would think he's taking them as usual. "There we are I'm ready."

"I'm ready," Alana said.

"Let's go," Sam told Alana as he walked towards the front door. He made sure to lock the dead bolt. The safety of his family was important; he always worried so much about them. He went to his truck and put his bag in and climbed into it and started it up and pulled out of the driveway slowly and was off to Vorgol's house.

"Does he know we're coming?"

"Yes and he has prepared the wards to protect

his inner sanctum. That's where he is waiting for us; he had set his traps well my love," Alana warned Sam.

"We have no choice, but to go at him head on," Sam grinned at the challenge set before him.

"Why are you smiling my dear?"

"This will be a test of our strength and we will win because it is a righteous fight."

"You're right my love," Alana said do her best to encourage Sam.

"Are we close yet?"

"Turn right at the next light darling."

"Okay."

"Then go up two blocks, his house is a red brick on the right."

"Got it," Sam said making a right turn at the traffic light.

He looked over at Alana and noticed her form shimmered silver and then gold. "What are you doing?"

"Preparing my love," she smiled.

"Everything will be okay," Sam promised.

"There," Alana pointed to Vorgol's house. "We won't have to worry about the first floor. The wards are set to trigger alone the stairwell leading down to his sanctum. We should be able to withstand the force blows and the concussive walls of pressure. Remember he is the master of the air element and his attacks will be air based, but make no mistake they are deadly," she said.

"Thanks Alana, you have done an excellent job, let's go pay him a visit," Sam smiled wildly.

Alana could tell Sam was primed for the fight. Sam looked up and down the street before getting out of his truck. And then walked around the back of it and got a pair of gloves out of the bag of things he bought at the super center on their way over. Then he got out a crowbar in case the door was locked. He walked on around to the passenger side and got into his overnight bag and pulled out his Desert Eagle semi-automatic pistol. He released the clip that he loaded earlier with hollow point bullets for maximum damage.

"What's that?" Alana ask.

"Back up if we need it, I don't want to kill him here if I can help it."

"The sanctum is sound proof, no one will hear us."

"That's good if things go bad," Sam said as he walked up the sidewalk leading up to the front porch. He slowly and silently walked up the steps and to the front door and checked in to see if it was unlocked. It wasn't, damn it Vorgol was definitely expecting him. Sam hated walking into an enemy's lair when they had time to prepare, the fight would be twice as deadly.

"Here goes nothing," Sam said though gritted teeth as he opened the front door.

"I'm right here my love."

Sam took a few seconds to scan the front room of the house which was sparsely furnished. The place was dark and the only light was coming through was the street light. He could see a door directly in front of him.

"Is that it?" Sam ask Alana.

"Yes," Alana answered.

Sam walked slowly and silently up to it again it was locked just like the front door, damn he thought.

"There's no turning back now," Sam whispered.

Alana remained silent followed Sam closely.

"Where are the wards Alana?" Sam ask again making sure he was right.

"Hallway my love," Alana said following down the stairs. "They are set to go off by any physical or spiritual presence."

"Okay," Sam said as he got to the bottom step, he took a deep breath and then stepped into the hallway and immediately the first ward exploded with an ear busting concussive blow that threw him against the opposite wall.

It took Sam a few seconds to shake it off,

thank god for Marlena's blessings otherwise he'd been extremely hurt. It was like a grenade going off right next to you, but with a stronger pressure wave.

"Damn," Sam said surprised by the force. He moved forward a few more steps and was stopped by an invisible wall in front of him with another invisible wall behind him moving towards him trying to squish him in between them like a vise. Suddenly a golden light came from him and destroyed the invisible walls. Once he was released he walked right into the next ward that caused a blast of rushing air that stopped him in his tracks and nearly knocked him backwards.

"One more my love," Alana told him as the air died down.

He made it a little further before going caught in what seemed a vacuum strong enough to take his breath away. He saw glowing sparkles surround him and expand outwards and the vacuum died.

"That was the last ward. We must deal with him quickly or he will destroy us both."

"Got it," Sam said as he stepped into the sanctum. The floor, walls, and ceiling were filled with symbols. There was an altar at the farthest end of the room were light gray smoke was swirling around it as filling the room making it difficult to see clearly. So much so that he couldn't see Vorgol.

"Welcome Samuel Stout!" Came a booming voice out of nowhere.

"Show yourself Victor!" Sam challenged.

"Come in, come to your death!" Vorgol bellowed.

Sam took another step in and was met by an invisible wall. "Alana can you break the barrier?"

"My pleasure my love," Alana said coming up beside him. "Step back darling."

Sam stepped back; Alana raised both arms high over her head and brought them down hard against the invisible wall. It sounded like a clap of thunder.

"It's down," Alana said as her form shimmered silver.

"You okay?"

"Yes, let move fast."

They both moved towards the altar expecting to find Vorgol behind it and was surprised to find him not there.

"Fools!" Came the voice again.

"Come out and face me!" Sam yelled angrily as he gripped his pistol, thinking this wasn't going to be a fight he could win with his fists.

To your left Sam," Alana said moving quickly in front of him. Suddenly silvery gray arrows materialized and soared directly at them. Alana spread her arms out and produced a shimmering shield in front of them causing the arrows to bounce off harmlessly.

"You'll have to do better than that Vorgol," Alana said fiercely.

Suddenly a rush of wind came from behind them knocking them off their feet. Sam and Alana slowly got to their feet fighting hard against the wind. Alana brought her arms up in front of her and moved them in a circular motion and then pushed forward. The wind dissipated as quickly as it had begun.

"Face me coward!" Sam yelled once more.

The sanctum grew quiet and then Vorgol stepped out of the shadows at the entrance of the chamber.

"Finally someone worthy to face me," Vorgol smiled as he took a step towards them.

"What do you say; just me and you, or do you need your little spirit bitch to help you?" Vorgol said menacingly.

"I'll face you gladly; I don't need any help to deal with you," Sam grinned wickedly taking a step towards Vorgol.

"NO!" Alana yelled out. SAM NO!" But it was too late, Sam charged at him.

Vorgol was ready and dodged his attempt, and then turned and struck Sam in his rib cage. Sam let out a howl of pain that doubled him over and took his breath for a second.

"NO ALANA!" Sam yelled seeing her coming to his aid. Alana stopped.

"Sam please," Alana begged.

"NO!" Sam said resolutely as rage induced adrenaline flooded his body. "He's mine," Sam bellowed as he regained his footing and charged back at Vorgol. This time connecting with a body block taking them both off their feet and crashed to the ground. Sam unloaded a flurry of fists to Vorgol's midsection casing him to let out a scream of pain. However Vorgol wrestled his way free of Sam's grip getting to his feet first he swiftly kicked Sam across his face causing him to nearly fall again, yet he regained his balance and prepared for the next vicious attack from Vorgol.

"Enough playing around," Vorgol growled as he worked his hands in a strange motion.

"You can't beat me with your unless magic," Sam retorted.

You'll see," Vorgol seethed working his hands faster and faster.

"SAM!" Alana yelled from behind him. "NO!" she screamed, before he knew it he was surrounded by a silvery glow. The next few seconds seemed like an eternity. A wall of force struck Sam like a runaway truck and knocked him backwards a few feet, luckily he managed to stay on his feet the whole time. Then what looked like smoky arrows flew fast, directly at him yet they dissipated upon striking him. He turned to look at Alana who was slumped over, her form blinking in and out.

"I told you no."

"Better me than you my love," Alana said weakly.

Sam felt a rage well up inside him as never before. He drew his Desert Eagle pistol and fired repeated at Vorgol yet the bullets stopped mid-air in front of him. Sam took the advantage of Vorgol having to focus his energy on stopping the bullets and took one last charge at him. This time Vorgol was not prepared for Sam's onslaught. Sam connected with a haymaker and then punched him in the stomach. He could feel Vorgol wither, yet he never let up continuing to deliver blow after blow until Vorgol was nearly half dead. Finally Sam came to his senses and stopped, he pulled out the zip ties from his back pocket and bound Vorgol's hands and feet so that he would be incapable of resisting. Then Sam's attention went back to Alana who appeared faintly.

"You okay?"

"Yes my love, I will be stronger once Vorgol has met his fate.

"He will shortly," Sam said still feeling the adrenaline running wild through his veins. "I need to go to my truck to get some bleach, there's blood on the floor."

Sam went out to his truck and got the bleach making sure that no one was around. He thought for sure that some of the noise had got out and alerted one of the neighbors, but it hadn't.

He went back down to the sanctum and poured bleach wherever he saw any blood splatter making it impossible to get and DNA from it, Vorgol was still out cold. Sam took one more look over the sanctum to make sure he hadn't missed anything. The last thing he needed was to be connected with Vorgol's disappearance.

"Okay," Sam said to Alana. "We are ready to go." Sam then bent down and picked up Vorgol and threw him over his shoulder and felt stinging pain in his right ribs, he knew he had cracked or broken ribs; however he didn't have time for that. Right now he had to get Vorgol taken care of. He carried Vorgol up the stairs grunting every time sharp pains shot through his ribs.

He stopped at the front door and looked up and down the street for any signs of approaching cars or any people, but at this hour few would be out of doors; most in their beds on this cool fall night. It was just what Sam needed to get his job done without any witnesses. He got to his pickup truck and threw Vorgol's limp body into the truck bed and then climbed into the bed so he could wrap Vorgol in a tarp so he wouldn't be seen by anyone. Sam had gagged him so he wouldn't be able to scream for help. He figured he wouldn't even if he could, thinking he would be able to get himself out of this situation. That was Vorgol's mistake, too much pride, Sam thought as he finished tying him up in the tarp. Sam climbed out of the truck bed and went back into the house to collect the bleach and do one last recon.

"Ready?" Sam ask Alana.

"Yes my love," she said in a weak voice.

"Anything I can do?"

"Just take care of Vorgol, I'll be strong once he is dead," Alana told Sam attempting a smile.

"Let's go," and with that Sam led Alana out to the truck. The city blurred as he sped to the old steel mill doing his best to drive the speed limit so he wouldn't get pulled by the police working the graveyard shift. Now that the adrenaline was fading, Sam's pain raced throughout his body; even though he was use to it the pain was crippling.

"My love you are hurt bad. I'm sorry I'm too weak to heal," Alana said sadly.

"I'll be okay," Sam clenched his jaws tightly.

"When Vorgol is gone I'll be strong enough to heal you."

"Okay," Sam said struggling to stay on top of the pain threatening to overtake him. Finally they arrived at the old mill; Sam slumped over the steering wheel. He could feel his strength leaving, yet he knew he must finish the task at hand. Alana laid a hand on his right shoulder and a surge of energy went through him.

"It's all I have," Alana's ghostly voice said.

She was so faint that Sam could barely see her.

"Alana stop you'll destroy yourself. I need you, please I cannot do it without you," Sam pleaded.

"I'll be okay my love, just finish Vorgol."

"Okay," Sam said getting out of his truck using his new found strength to wrestle Vorgol out of the tarp and unto his shoulder and carried him into the old abandoned mill where he would meet his doom. By the time Sam got to him to where the crucible was Vorgol began to stir.

"Don't let him speak, he will summon air spirits to attack us," Alana's came weak but clear.

"Don't worry I won't let this bastard speak one word," Sam said as he lit the burners and moved the old crucible over them. Then Sam moved around behind Vorgol and snipped his thumbs off sending him withering in pain.

"Now you son-of-a-bitch maybe you can feel a little of the pain you inflicted upon those innocent victims. Be sure to say hi to your comrades in hell," Sam told him as he hoisted him above the iron crucible and without wasting any time lowered him in. At least there wasn't any screaming this time, just silence as Sam sat down and watched it for a minute and saw air swirling at the top of the kettle like a small tornado. The surge of strength he got from Alana now dying.

"Be still my love," Alana's voice now stronger.

Sam knew he was hurt far worse than he had originally thought.

"I can heal you enough to get to Marlena's. She can completely heal you," Alana spoke softly and she moved her hands in a circle over Sam's chest. He cried out in pain as the broken ribs reset themselves.

"I'm sorry my love I know you are in pain."

"I'm okay," Sam said through clenched teeth.

Alana moved her hands over his stomach. He felt a sharp pain that caused him to see spots.

"That will stop the internal bleeding for a little while. We have to work fast though," Alana's voice had a sense of urgency to it.

"I just need to drop Vorgol's ashes off and then we can go to Marlena's. I'm feeling better," Sam told Alana and looked at his watch. "Damn it's already four am I won't be able to make it to Cleveland on time. I'll call Jim so he can cover for me," Sam said.

He thought of the feeling he had of finally getting closer to the one responsible for his sister's death and achieving justice. Sam went over to the gas valve and turned it up and watched the mesmerizing flames lick up the sides of the already red hot crucible. He had to get it done quickly looking at his watch again, four thirty am, he cursed quietly to himself. Sam sat back down feeling nauseous.

"My love be still, all is well," Alana spoke

softly.

Sam grimaced, "I know love, we will win this fight, and together we cannot be stopped."

He waited another hour before shutting off the gas; the flames flickered and went out. The crucible cooled down enough for him to shovel the ashes into a metal bucket. He carried them out to his truck and placed them inside the cab. Then he got into his glove box and opened the prepaid cell phone he had bought earlier that day. He carried a notebook of important names and phone numbers. He looked up Jim's and called him making up a story about his truck breaking down on the way to Cleveland and had to have it towed to a garage. He was waiting for it to open so he could get it fixed. One good thing about being the boss is employees don't question you. Even though he trusted Jim with his life he would not bring him into this, this was his war.

Sam fired up his truck and headed for downtown, this time he had something different in mind to do with the ashes. He was going to leave them at the Columbus Reader newspaper and then head for Marlena's. It was a cool morning, but Sam was sweating profusely, he knew it was because of the internal damage he suffered in the fight with Vorgol. Alana saw this and laid her hand on his shoulder. Sam felt an easing of the pain.

"Hurry my love," Alana pleaded.

"It won't take a few minutes to drop the ashes," Sam told her as he turned a corner a little too fast and fish-tailed before he got it under control, thankfully no one was around to see. Alana kept her hand on his shoulder feeding healing energy into Sam's wounded body.

We're here," he told her as he parked the truck near the front entrance and got the ashes out of the truck bed and walked up to the front door of the newspaper. He piled them up and placed the letter and thumb on top of it, and then returned to the truck and headed for Marlena's which wasn't far away.

This time Sam parked in the back so if someone came they wouldn't see his truck. He knocked on the back door and waited and before long he saw Marlena through the glass in the door.

She opened it, "Sam your hurt," she said with panic in her voice, "come in, come in," she grabbed his arm, "oh you're hurt bad," she said leading him into the living room and got him to lay down on the couch.

"It will be just a minute dear, I need to get a few things," she said and disappeared from sight. Sam finally relaxed and that's when it hit him with the adrenaline gone the pain now ran like lightning throughout his body, blackness now invaded his mind and over took him. He was teleported to a magical place, beings in white robes and golden colored skin floated past him. If they would have had wings they could have been angels Sam thought as he drifted in between consciousness.

Chapter 19 After

Sleep was swift and sound; the alarm was an unwelcome interruption as Sarah rolled over and smacked the snooze button and then rolled back over to cuddle up to James who barely stirred. Finally after hitting the snooze button a second time it was time to get up. She gently rubbed his shoulder, "time to get up sleepy head," she said softly.

"Morning," James said still trying to get his bearings.

"How did you sleep?"

"Great, just wish we could have slept in. Maybe after we get this case solved we will."

"Sounds great," she smiled and gave him a quick kiss and then he grabbed her and passionately kissed her.

"Now, now handsome, get dressed we got a

killer to catch," she told him pulling away.

"Yes ma'am, Detective Colburn on the case, reporting for duty," he smiled as he got his clothes on.

They both got dressed and headed out.

"Damn six am, we got to hurry and get to Marlena's. The briefing will start at eight am sharp and I don't want Captain Harris to have our asses if we show up late. And don't forget to act normal around everyone at the precinct," Sarah instructed.

"No problem," James said as he opened the car door for her.

"That's what I'm talking about; I love your chivalry, but don't do that at work."

"Sorry it's a habit," James sighed.

"Unless you want to be writing parking tickets the rest of your life you better not get us caught," Sarah warned him in a stern tone, yet he kept smiling.

"I promise I will treat you like any other person when we are working," James said solemnly.

"Good, now let's go, times a wasting," Sarah said as James walked around to the driver's side of his car and got in and started it up and they headed for Marlena's.

"Do you think we need to get a search warrant?" James ask.

"There's not a chance in hell of getting one simply based on our suspicions," Sarah answered and then continued, "besides now that we know more I'll know if she's lying to me, but we have to find a connection between her and the Avox."

"Or she may be covering for her son's past involvement."

"Good point."

"Or perhaps hers; how well do you know her?" James ask making a turn onto High Street.

"Not well enough to know whether or not she's involved, but we are damn sure going to find out," Sarah looked dead serious at him. "Turn right up here."

"Got it, let's just be careful she may more than a simple bag of tricks up her sleeve."

"Oh now James you're not scared of a little old lady, are you?" Sarah laughed.

"The innocent looking ones are always the most dangerous ones," James defended himself.

"I agree, left at the next light."

Finally they pulled into the front of Marlena's house. James absentmindedly checked his service weapon.

"Don't get trigger happy there cowboy. Let me take the lead in there and remember this is my area of expertise. I'll know if she's telling the truth."

"It's not the truth I'm worried about. If she is involved in this Avox group it means she's not alone and now that she knows you're on to her she'll be ready. I don't take any chances," James said firmly getting out of the car.

"Like I said, follow my lead," Sarah warned him. She had been around her share of trigger-happy cops and it never ended well.

She walked up to the front door and knocked loudly. It was dark inside, she knocked again and saw a side door open of the front parlor open and a light came on.

"Hello again detectives; how may I help you?" Marlena ask.

"We just have a few follow up questions if you don't mind?" Sarah ask.

"It's not a good time, I'm sorry I'm not feeling well."

"It won't take long after all I do prefer to do it here instead of down at the station," Sarah said firmly.

Marlena got the point, "well then come in."

James took a quick look around the place; he couldn't shake the uneasy feeling he had in the pit of his stomach. His hand kept going to his holstered pistol unconsciously. Sarah saw it and gave him a look.

"Please sit, now how can I help you

detectives?" Marlena ask.

"We have a reliable source that you may be aware of a group called the Avox operating in the city," Sarah said not beating around the bush.

So much for warming up to her James thought.

"Like I told you detectives I keep to myself and what few clients I have wouldn't be mixed up in anything like that," Marlena said sweetly, which made Sarah even angrier.

"I'm not here to play games with you Marlena, it's a matter of time before we find out if you or your son was involved," Sarah said steely.

The smile dropped from Marlena's face and any pretense of civility left.

"Listen Detective Breckenridge never soil the name of my son again; neither he, nor I would ever be associated with any scum to which you are talking about," Marlena spat to her left.

This was exactly what Sarah wanted, to anger Marlena and get to the truth.

"So you do know about the Avox? If you are not with them then why hide the fact that you know about them? Are you afraid of them? Sarah ask.

"It isn't them you need to be afraid of detective," Marlena smiled.

"Is that a threat?" This time it was James asking.

"James I got this," Sarah called him down.

"You should only wish it was a threat," Marlena looked directly at James as if to challenge him.

"Listen here old woman I'm not scared of your useless witchcraft…" James started but was cut off by Sarah.

"James go outside and wait," she told him. He hesitated. "Now!" Sarah said in a loud voice.

"Okay, okay, I'll be right outside the door," James said angrily.

"Your mental games won't work on me Marlena. You should know better," Sarah told her.

"Your mistake is thinking I'm playing games," Marlena's face changed suddenly.

"NO!" Marlena yelled and in a split second the side door to the parlor flew open. It was Sam.

"Alana get him back in there!" Marlena commanded in a much deeper tone which surprised Sarah who got to her feet in an instant.

"He's not well, we disturbed him that's all," Marlena said getting up and moved in front of him.

"Marlena get out of the way," Sarah commanded pulling her pistol out.

"No, you don't know what you doing! Please stop, he's sick, I've been treating him," Marlena pleaded.

By this time James came through the front door with his weapon drawn.

"Easy James we got this, everyone just take it easy," Sarah said trying to get a handle on the tense situation, but it was too late.

"GUN!" James yelled as he saw Sam pull his weapon from behind Marlena and point it at Sarah.

"Everyone…" was the last word Sarah got out before all hell broke loose. James saw Sarah's body flying backwards, everything went into slow motion. He fired trying to hit Sam, yet was mortified to see the shocked look on Marlena's face as she clutched her chest and fell to the floor.

"OH GOD NO!" James screamed, but before he could fire off another round at Sam, he felt a lightning hot round pierce his right ribs and explode inside him. He managed to fire off another shot as he fell onto his back clutching his ribs. Darkness crept into his mind, he was drifting into blackness, muffled sounds; his last thought was Sarah.

She didn't know how long she had been

out; it could have been minutes or hours. Everything was so fuzzy, she felt like she had been hit by a truck. She sat up slowly checking herself for any gunshot wounds; she was okay except the dull ache in her head. Then she realized the carnage that had taken place. Marlena was dead and then it struck her; James, oh God! She didn't want to look but she had to. He was lying just inside the door on his back in a pool of blood. She crawled over to him, he was still breathing shallow. She looked at the wound; it was bad at the right side of his ribs.

"James please stay with me," she pleaded as she tore her shirt to make a makeshift bandage to stop the bleeding. James please, if you can hear me please fight, stay with me."

She grabbed her cell phone with her free hand and called 911.

"This is Detective Breckenridge, I have an officer down, shots fired, please help," she just kept saying over and over. Mentally she was doing her best to get a hold of herself. Why, oh why did she sleep with him? Why did she cross that line? It was too late for why's, now was the time for action. Her brain frantically trying for remember the details while staying on the blood soaked phone.

"James please wake up, you have to be okay," she told him while holding pressure on his wound. He was fading fast, there was so much blood.

"HOW MUCH LONGER?" She screamed into the phone.

"ETA four minutes on ambulance, officers should be on scene now," a woman's voice replied. All the while telling her to keep pressure on the wound and check his breathing. Sarah could hear the sirens wailing in the distance. She knew an officer down call would get every cop in the city on the lookout, but for whom? She was having trouble focusing everything happened so fast. Something came at her knocking her out so she never got a close look at who was being shielded by Marlena.

"Detective Breckenridge, we got him," it was a male voice that broke her concentration. "We got him," it was a paramedic joined by another working fast to move him onto a stretcher. She sat there still in shock of what had happened.

"Detective Breckenridge; Detective Breckenridge, are you okay?" said a male voice louder causing her to snap out of her daze.

"Yes, I'm okay, I'm not hurt just take care of Colburn," she said pushing their hands away and got shakily to her feet trying to muster all her strength.

"What did the shooter look like?"
This time it was a uniformed officer asking.
She knew it was important to act fast after a
shooting.

"White male; about six foot, dark brown
hair; I couldn't see what he was wearing," was
the only thing she remembered, why was her
memory affected? She always had an eye for
details.

"Did he have a get-a-way car?" the
officer asked.

"None in the front when we pulled up,
he must have parked in the back."

"Was the woman armed?"

"No, not that I saw, I was knocked out
before Detective Colburn came through the
door. The man must have been armed and
Colburn pulled out his service weapon when
he saw me go down and fired on him," Sarah
said.

"We'll get CSU in here and every cop in
the city is on this. Are you okay? Do you want
to go to the hospital to check on Colburn?"
The officer ask.

"Yes I am, notify me if you find
anything, also please have a sketch artist meet
me at the hospital so we can get a description
of our suspect. Also check the back of the
house and see if you can find any tire tracks

that we can get a mold of," Sarah instructed the uniformed officer.

"Yes ma'am," the officer replied and then went about his work.

Sarah went out and got into James' unmarked cruiser, the keys were still in the ignition. She fired it up and hit the lights and siren and sped away. The city was a blur; it was a miracle she made it to the hospital in one piece. She went to the emergency room.

"Detective James Colburn," the words burned her heart. "Where did they take him?" She choked back tears. "I'm Detective Breckenridge his partner."

"He's in emergency surgery, please have a seat and I'll get a status update for you," the young brown haired nurse said. Yet Sarah was too wired up to sit and instead paced back and forth. It seemed like an eternity before a different nurse with red hair came to her.

"Are you Detective Breckenridge?"

"Yes, how is he?"

"Right now its touch and go he lost a lot of blood. The bullet has done extensive internal damage. He'll be in surgery for a few more hours. I'll update you as soon as I can."

"Please," Sarah looked at her in tears.

"Don't worry he's in good hands, I promise I'll be the first one to tell you when they've been a change," the nurse said reassuringly.

"Thank you," Sarah said trying to pull herself together. She was shaking when she pulled her phone out. She knew she had to call her father he would hear about her being in a shoot out and be worried.

"Hi dad, yes," she couldn't get out much over him talking.

"I'm fine, don't worry, yes I'm at the hospital with Detective Colburn. I'll let you know if they catch the guy who done it and I'll update you on Colburn as soon as I can. I know I got to go, love you bye," Sarah said before hanging up.

She found the coffee machine and got her a hot cup, anything to distract her while waiting. She kept playing the scene over and over in her mind. She should have handled in differently; this was her fault, he was a rookie detective. Damn it, damn it, over and over, why. There was no undoing this, he had to live, he just had to. What would she do if he didn't make it? She couldn't let herself to think like that. Stay positive she told herself, stay in control, once he's okay they would track down the son-of-a-bitch that done this.

Her next call was to Captain Harris.

"Captain, this is Breckenridge, Colburn's been shot. He's in surgery now, I'll update you as soon as there's been a change," she tried to keep it short.

"Yes Captain, understood, thank you," she said and hung up. She knew he would notify the next of kin. Hours went by; she went back up to the desk.

"Anything?" she asked the same brown haired nurse.

"I'll check ma'am," she said and disappeared down the long hallway.

While she was gone Captain Harris came in with a woman and a man, from the looks of it, it was James' parents. Both were wiping away tears. Harris saw Breckenridge.

"Mr. and Mrs. Colburn this is Detective Breckenridge, James' partner," Captain Harris introduced them.

"Hello," was all they could manage. They could see the redness in her eyes and her pain.

"How is he?" they asked.

"The nurse just went to check on his condition and will be back in a moment," Sarah told them choking on her words.

Captain Harris put his hand on her shoulder. "Everything will be okay," he did his best to comfort her, yet all she wanted was to hold James in her arms again one more time. She had butterflies in her stomach and felt nauseous when she saw the red-headed nurse who spoke to her earlier coming down the hallway.

"Hello Detective Breckenridge," she said.

Sarah introduced James' parents and Captain Harris.

"He's out of surgery," you could hear an audible sigh of relief.

"However the next twenty-four hours will be critical, we had to give him a transfusion of blood and repair the damage to his internal organs, his liver is badly damaged. If he makes it through the night, he may survive. He's being moved to the critical care unit now, you'll be able to see him soon," she told them.

"Let's all sit, it's going to be a long night," Captain Harris suggested and they went over to the waiting area too grief stricken to speak.

Sarah saw Harris go over to the corner to speak on his cell phone.

"Detective Breckenridge, a word please," Harris ask.

"CSU has pulled a half dozen prints

from the scene and pieces of a slug from the wall. It will take a little time to run the prints, but the slug was too damaged for ballistics. Is there anything else you can tell me about the man?" Harris ask gently.

"Nothing that I can remember, just what I told the officer at the scene," Sarah replied.

"So far they've searched the area and found no one on foot; he couldn't have gone far on foot. He had to be in a vehicle, we have a chopper in the air to see if any cars were leaving the scene and also any vehicles in the general area. However it's a long shot by now, they've been too much time past. We're also checking all traffic cams in a five block radius around the time the shooting took place to see if any cars were leaving from the house," Captain Harris brought her up to speed.

"Thank you Captain, thank you for everything your doing. I should have handled things better, it's my fault," Sarah said.

"It's not your fault, quit blaming yourself and blame the suspect; he's the one who will pay. No one shoots one of my own and gets by with it. I need you to do me a favor," Harris ask.

"Anything," Sarah answered without hesitation.

"Tell your father I need to commandeer two of the news helicopters so we can widen the search area so this bastard doesn't get away," Harris ask.

"Done," Sarah grabbed her phone and was already dialing.

"Dad Captain Harris needs two news choppers in the air now, look for any suspicious vehicles from First and Fifth Streets to High Street, which may be abandoned by now. Report to local authorities on the ground, thanks dad," she hung up the phone.

"Anything else Captain?" she ask.

"Yes, pray, pray that Colburn pulls through he may be our only hope in solving this damn case," Harris said solemnly before walking over to James' parents.

"We have every man available on finding out who was responsible for this; we will get him," Harris promised,

They just sat there huddled in silence in tears fearing the worst. Sarah wanted to offer words of comfort, but was barely able to hold herself together. Finally the nurse came back.

"He's been moved, you can see him now, but only one at a time," the nurse told them.

They followed her down the long hallway and finally came to the critical care room. Sarah waited until his parents went in, each of which came out in tears streaming down their face. This stirred her emotions even more and then she went in. There he lay on the hospital bed with a tube down his throat and so many wires and an IV she nearly broke down just looking at him. How could a night of bliss turn into a daytime of gut wrenching hell. She slowly walked over to him and held his hand and gently kissed his forehead, tears flowed freely down her cheeks, and she didn't try to stop them.

"James," she whispered, "you have to get better, fight, fight to come back to me. You can do it; I believe in you, you are strong." She kissed his forehead again, "I'll be strong for you," she finished and wiped away her tears. She had to find a way to turn them into determination to help him anyway she could and the first thing was to find the bastard who done this to him.

With that she left the room and resigned herself to stay at the hospital until he woke up. So she went back out to the waiting room to rejoin his parents. Captain Harris had already left having too much to take care of to stay behind. She went to get another coffee and back to sit and wait which was the hardest part. The uncertainty of whether or not James would ever wake up.

The scenes flashed repeatedly through her mind, the blood, the feeling of helplessness. She had to hold it together only she could solve this case. She knew one person to check with who could provide more insight now that she had more to go on and that was Victor Vorgol; he was her only hope. She pulled out her phone there was still dried blood on it. She tried to wipe in off but in wouldn't come off, she would leave it there as a reminder of the importance of her mission. There was no answer; she tried again, still no answer, so she left an urgent voice message. Damn it she thought as she went to put her phone up it rang, it was the Captain.

"Have you seen the news?" Harris ask.

"No, why?" Sarah ask.

"They've been another one," Harris said.

"What?" Sarah ask still in shock.

"This time the Vendetta Killer has left the ashes at the Columbus Reader newspaper. It was found this morning by an employee at five-thirty a.m. It's all over the news, the bastards never called us until they had it on the channel five newscast. CSU is there now," Harris said.

"Same M.O.?" Sarah ask.

"Yes," Harris answered.

"What's the victim's name?" Sarah ask.

"Victor Vorgol, but we haven't confirmed the identity yet," Harris replied.

Sarah nearly dropped her phone.

"Hello?" Harris said after she went silent.

"What's wrong?" Harris ask.

"Oh nothing, I thought I saw the nurse again," she lied. "Is there anything I can do?"

"Stay close to Colburn, the Vendetta Killer may try to get to him and finish the job. I'm sending over two uniforms to post a security. Watch your back you may be on the list now to," Harris told her.

Deep down she wished the son-of-a-bitch would try her so she could get even over what happened to James.

"Any update on Colburn?" Harris ask.

"Not yet Captain, I'll call you first thing as soon as anything changes," Sarah said.

"Thanks," Harris said and hung up.

It was like her worst nightmare was coming true. She knew and spent untold hours talking to him about ancient religion, surly she would have known if he was a killer, wouldn't she? After all the Vendetta Killer was only going after serial killers and Victor couldn't be one or could he? She felt sick to her stomach; her world was turning upside down. Surly Victor will turn up alive, maybe this time the Vendetta Killer had made a mistake and killed the wrong man. She had to know, but she couldn't leave James so she got on her phone and called the M.E.'s office to see which CSU team had been sent out to the scene. She talked to the lead crime scene investigator there. It was identical to the previous three.

"Has anyone checked his residence? Please call me as soon as they get on scene," Sarah ask.

God the waiting was killing her, she tried Victor's number again, damn voicemail. Come on, finally her phone rang.

"This is Special Agent Tim Norton with the FBI forensics team we're here at Victor Vorgol's residence. It looks like all hell broke loose; we won't know anything for a while. However there are no bodies at the scene that we can find. We are in the process of securing the scene and I'll be in touch as soon as I have something to report," Norton told her.

"Thanks," was the only thing that Sarah could say before hanging up. How could she have been so blind? How could she have missed the clues, surly they were there? Maybe she wasn't the detective she thought she was. Her world was falling apart. God she needed James to pull through. He was the only man she had let in, in so long. It made her so angry, if she hadn't she wouldn't be in so much pain right now on top of the confusion about Victor. Minutes turned into hours, there was so much she needed to be doing, but there was no way in hell she was going to leave the hospital until she knew James was out of danger. She dozed off finally into fitful dreams of mixed scenes of Victor and then James, back and forth.

"Miss; are you Detective Breckenridge?" this time it was a blond haired nurse with glasses.

"Yes," Sarah answered.

"Detective Colburn is awake and asking for you," she said.

"Has his parents been in to see him?" Sarah ask.

"Yes they just left to get some rest. It looks like you could use some to, these chairs aren't comfortable," the nurse said.

"I'm okay; what time is it?" Sarah ask.

"Two a.m., I'll take you to him. He's still in the critical care unit, hopefully we can move him to a regular room soon," the nurse informed her.

Sarah couldn't be happier it felt like a giant weight had been lifted off her chest as she followed the nurse down the hallway. She took a deep breath before entering his room.

"Boy you're a sight for sore eyes," James said weakly.

"Shh don't talk, you need your strength," Sarah told him.

"I'm okay, just weak."

"You lost a lot of blood."

"From what I hear you saved my life."

She held his hands; they felt so warm in hers.

"I thought I lost you," Sarah said tearing up.

"It's okay, I'm here," James comforted her. She gently laid her head upon his chest, he stroked her long hair. "I'm here I won't leave you," he promised.

"I'll find the one responsible," Sarah vowed.

"It's funny; I don't remember anything after opening the door. I've been trying so hard, but I can't," James said.

"It's okay, it will come back. Thank god you're alive," she kissed his lips and held his face in her soft hands.

Chapter 20 Convergence

Sam could hear voices, but he couldn't understand what they were saying or where they were coming from. Was he dreaming? Was this part of Marlena's healing? He tried to move, but couldn't, he was paralyzed. He tried to talk, but no words came out. He hated feeling helpless. He tried harder, "Alana," came out barely above a whisper. "Alana, come to my aid my love, do not forsake me," he managed.

"I'm here my love, I'll never forsake you. You must let Marlena heal you. You have internal bleeding; she must staunch it for you to survive."

"Okay," Sam said in a whisper before blackness consumed him. He could feel heat radiating throughout his body from his head to his feet. Wave after wave pulsated up and down, he could feel himself growing stronger.

"It's almost complete dear," Marlena said.

Then more voices drew him into a calm place deep within himself, everything went quiet and he at peace. He lay there on the old couch at rest until he heard different voices. This time he heard Marlena then another woman followed by a man raising his voice. Suddenly Sam sat straight up as if in a trance, then got to his feet slowly and nearly fell backwards, but managed to stay upright.

"Sam no!" Alana begged, but it sounded like Marlena was in trouble, he had to act. He walked over and opened the door leading to the front parlor. Marlena ran to him and stood in front of him shielding him from the monsters coming for him.

"ALANA HELP ME!" Sam yelled.

Alana threw all her energy at the woman threatening Marlena knocking her backwards to the floor. A man burst through the front door with a weapon.

"SAM!," Alana yelled, but Sam was already drawing his pistol and fired, but not fast enough the unknown man got off two shots one striking Marlena.

"NO!" Sam screamed as she fell

forward clutching her chest.

"No! No! Please Alana heal her, help her," Sam yelled trying to stop the bleeding.

"Please don't die, you can't leave me, we're not finished, I need you!" Sam pleaded. He knew Marlena was gone and there wasn't anything him or Alana could do to change that, he reluctantly left.

"We'll come back my love," Alana promised.

"It's not over," Sam ground his teeth together. He hated leaving Marlena like that, but he knew cops would be swarming the place soon. He got into his truck and sped away.

Once he came to himself and realized that they weren't monsters coming at him but two people he asked Alana, "were they the same two cops that had been there before?"

"Yes."

"Why did they come back?"

"They found information about the Avox from Madam Andrea."

"Do they know about us?"

"No."

"We'll have to lie low for a little while," Sam said slowing down after seeing police

cars with lights and sirens heading towards
Marlena's place he was sure. He had to think,
he was supposed to be in Cleveland. He turned
onto two-seventy north toward Cleveland, he
would go a little ways and call Jim and let him
know that he was still getting his truck worked
on. He knew he had to ditch the gun and get a
hold of Jacquelyn to let her know he would be
home earlier than planned. He drove in silence
for a while and pulled over at a rest area. How
could he have messed up things so bad and
jump the gun and cause the death of Marlena
and possibly two others.

So many questions were going through
him mind, they must have figured out that
Marlena had a connection to him.

"Rest easy my love they do not know
about you," Alana told him seeing him
thoughts.

"Are you sure?"

"Yes love," Alana reassured him.

"We must get to Logar as soon as things
calm down a little bit."

"Don't worry; with Marlena gone her
power has entered into me until another Nabila
is chosen."

"How will we know?"

"When the time has come I will know,
but for now let's concentrate on Logar."

"And finally have justice for my sister," Sam said getting out his phone.

"Jim this is Sam, I won't be able to make it up there today. I'll have the office secretary fax up what needs to be done and meet with dad to get a progress report," Sam informed him. Now it was time to call Jacquelyn.

"Hi babe."

"Is everything okay? I've been worried about you. I talked to Jim earlier and he told me you had car trouble and didn't make it to Cleveland."

"It's okay, I just got off the phone with him and my truck is nearly fixed. I'll be home soon and get some rest."

"Okay babe please be careful, I wish you would get a new truck, that thing's so old," Jacquelyn said in her motherly tone.

"Just like me," Sam said with laugh.

"Just get home in one piece."

"I will, love you."

"Love you to."

Now that was taken care of Sam could concentrate on Logar.

"Do you know where he is?" Sam asked Alana.

"Now that the others are gone he is opened and exposed my love," Alana replied.

"Good."

"I'll go and see if he's at his sanctum."

Sam sat and waited at the rest area for a while until she returned.

"He's there, but the city is filled with police. It wouldn't be wise to attack him now," Alana informed Sam.

"I have special plans for him," Sam grinned as he started his truck and headed back to Columbus. He stopped by the river and got out concealing his pistol he strolled down to its bank. There wasn't anyone around; he carefully wiped it down so there would be no fingerprints. The he threw it as far as he could; it landed in the middle of the river with a splash. He hated getting rid of it, it was his favorite weapon, yet his mission was more important. He walked back up his truck and asked Alana, "How hard will Logar be to take down?"

"He is the strongest of the Avox and will be the most difficult to take down my love."

"Am I strong enough?"

"You will be I can bestow blessings upon you. Marlena's power now flows through me," Alana said as they got into the truck and headed home.

"Thank you."

"For what my love?"

"Just wanted to thank you for being here in my time of need."

"You're welcome my love, I would give my life for you. You are the sole reason I am here," Alana said placing her ghostly hand on Sam's shoulder. He felt that familiar tingling sensation. It made him feel so connected to Alana it was hard to explain. How could he feel so close to a spirit? He felt closer to her than he did most people, she understood him and his pain.

It wasn't too long before he was pulling into his driveway. Jacquelyn was at work and the kids were at school. He would have time to plan; however there would be no way of going out tonight cops would be all over the city.

Sam decided to turn on the news and see what was going on and if they had found Vorgol's ashes yet. Sure enough they did and also news of the shooting at Marlena's, thankfully they didn't have a good description of him. Just a white male; dark brown hair, approximately six feet tall which could be anybody. They also reported that Detective Colburn was in critical condition and Detective Breckenridge was okay.

"Alana will she remember anything else?" Sam ask.

"No; when I hit her I also blocked her memory," Alana said.

"Good, we have a chance of getting to Logar without them knowing it was me at Marlena's."

"Once the police leave her house we need to go back and retrieve her spirit shawl so I can bestow blessings upon you," Alana said.

"It will be dangerous for me to go back there. Can you get it?"

"I'll try my love; I will have to take physical form in order to get it."

"Are you able to do that?"

"With the additional power I have from Marlena I think I can, but I haven't tried yet."

"Try now and see otherwise I'll have to go with you."

Alana's form crackled with blue steaks of light like an electrical storm and then she materialized. This amazed Sam as he sat and watched Alana come to life.

"Wow," Sam exclaimed as her form shimmered and went back to her ghostly body.

"I may be able to last longer; I'll keep working hard it."

"You're amazing I'm sure you will be able to; now back to Logar. Where does he live?"

"He lives near where you had your accident Sam. One more thing Sam, he is the one responsible for Arlene's death your first physical therapist you had," Alana said solemnly.

"It's okay, I'm stronger now, and I can deal with it. However we must take him alive. It's the only way for me to have closure of my sister's death and avenge Arlene and the others he murdered."

"Together my love we will," Alana purred.